Face to the Reality

Laurent Tshimbeka

authorHOUSE®

AuthorHouse™
1663 Liberty Drive
Bloomington, IN 47403
www.authorhouse.com
Phone: 1 (800) 839-8640

Published by AuthorHouse   03/31/2016

ISBN: 978-1-5246-0131-7 (sc)
ISBN: 978-1-5246-0130-0 (e)

Print information available on the last page.

This book is printed on acid-free paper.

Epigraph

ABIBU, faced to the reality, is a symbol, an interpellation and an exhortation. It is the symbol of a disinherited people victim of social injustice of the political system of his country and who goes looking for an eldorado in other climes. It is also an interpellation, to anyone with a parcel of responsibility to act in human that should draw some useful lessons for equitable distribution of social justice among peoples, and finally an exhortation to the youth, disoriented and discouraged, do not lose hope but remain optimistic in order to build a better future.

Roger KOY BABES'IWA DIADIA
(Adviser)

The book FACE TO THE REALITY is a romance that tells the story of a people who suffered in their own country. It is a complicate and difficult story that relates the author through the journey of a young man, who from his childhood until his adulthood was a victim of the realities of his society. This work is a collection of true stories lived and heard by the author and he has seen fit to share with his readers. This romantic opus has a mission beyond what could be attributed to the common mortal. That is to say, this novel has a mission beyond its borders. A pedagogical task entrusted to him as an alarm bell to all segments of the world population.

The experience discussed in this book is not a simple abstraction but a true reality, experienced directly and indirectly by a young man named ABIBU the general personnality, living in sub-Saharan African countries characterized by absence of a strong political and unable to secure, protect and ensure the well being of the population. This results in social injustice, anarchy and the abandonment of the population to its own fate. A situation that benefits a minority of people at the expense of the vast majority of the population languishes in poverty.

Faced with such a crisis and an exaggerated carelessness which is explained by the absence of a rule of law, where everyone is a little bit of responsibility, and is without reigns supreme no sense of patriotism or human. The author is an eyewitness and victim of the realities of his country, by the fact that he is from a poor family belongs to the vast majority suffering.

That's why he speaks in this novel with the aim of urging anyone who may find themselves in the same situations as revealed its securities, not to despair but to continue to transcend, and those who seem to ignore for multiple reasons, the suffering of others, to sympathize with the misfortunes of others in one way or another through their acts of benevolence towards this marginalized class by the leaders of their country of origin and other countries, especially those of the great powers. In short, that each of us regardless of social class, race, education, membership in both social conscience for the welfare of all. That's how this romantic work is destined for you, read, read...

SECTION I

GETTING STARTED

TITLE I

THE DIVORCE

ABIBU is a boy of about five years living next to his grandmother with his cousins. He was accustomed to see his mom whose he called Yaya always moving towards travel and his dad came to visit him occasionally.

Every time he cast a glance at the neighbors, he saw his comrades beside their parents, that is to say closed to their dad and their mom constantly. This was not the case at their home and he did not understand. Embarrassed by the ardent desire to know such a clear situation that made him confused, he allows himself one day while they were around the fire looked like as usual at dusk with its own sun. He dared to ask his grandmother Màmà why are you raise us alone without Tàtà and why Tàtà does not live with us?

When ABIBU asked this question, he adopted a serious look. This attitude attracted the attention of her cousins who surrounded him. Suddenly Màmà was surprised by the overwhelming issue, she was sick at heart and she began to moan. A few minutes later, she shook the boy's head with a soft hand and reacts with all wisdom: ABIBU, ABIBU, ABIBU it is already too late, let's go to sleep, I'm tired by the toil of the day. Friendly he was, going away quietly ABIBU sleep with others. The next day, Mama woke up early and goes to tell the scene to an old man who she considered like one of the village elders before going about her business, because she knew the fate that awaited evening when she will return home. At the side of ABIBU, he woke up with the hope of being fulfilled his concern and in order to avoid loopholes in the other way yesterday night he has organized to supplement the work housewives often tired her grandmother.

The evening, after supper Mama after they found themselves all at the usual place and grandmother after several attempts to try to forget the young man. She realized that it was not so easy at the moment to forget to his little son folder

4

that has remained so attentive to his movements. That was how he decided to answer the question of the caller and based the response of sage she accessed morning. Speaking grandmother replied ABIBU my grandson, yesterday when you asked me this question, in which you want to know why am i raise you alone without Tàtà as you ever found elsewhere among our neighbors. If I did not want to answer you hinc and now, it was because your question has make me very upset, stop and shock.

To hear such a question from a boy you are, it made me cry, but maybe you have not found out and I avoided you see me cry because it would make you panic all. That's why I had invited you all to bed so that I may suffer this pain alone. My grandson ABIBU you know that very well I love you all very much because each of you still remind me a story or a happy and unhappy memories, good or bad of my life was not so easy until these days. That why I fight my body and my soul lest you do not suffer the same fate as me or unless your yaya. If I link your yaya in this suffering, it is because they have suffer too and if they don't have position today, it was due to the sudden death of your Tàtà. Your grand father was a nice guy full of etiquette, good manner, charisma and spirituality. Following his untimely death poison that had been his masuwa (comrades) who were jealous of his qualities, achievements and merits as military.

This unfortunate situation had destabilized his home which I was the manager. Girl I was at the time, it was a nightmare even the end of the world for me. I did not know where to start with children he had left me sole responsibility and especially that I was an only child, lost her father and mother. Me and my children have gone through difficult times, painful. A few days after the funeral of my husband, my family in low came to rob me all of little things that we have with my husband and they drove me out of home with my children. This practice was covered by our custom. Me and my children, we found ourselves under the stars. As my own parents were no longer alive, nobody in my family could not plead my case, even those that I regarded as close to my parents. All looking at me from afar without any reaction. Instead, they encouraged my sisters and brothers in low to make me suffer. All because I refused the husband who had been previously proposed, forced by my uncles and aunts family before I married my late husband. He had suggested that there was a village elder who had his livestock, large tracts of farmland and many workers.

My family push me to marry with the old man the age of deceased father because my family was attracted by his wealth. While I was looking for a husband of my age with whom we would form our home. So I rejected their offer to tie me to my late husband. But since this refusal, they kept a grudge against me. While my husband was still alive, all pretended to love us, but in reality it was only farce and hypocrisy. This refusal was for them a sign of disobedience that I expressed to them, whereas in all I was looking for my happiness, not wealth they envied.

In the mentality of the people of our time, enter into a marriage with a village elder was a sign of honor and prestige behind it because the family would enjoy many material and social benefits. Refuse such an opportunity was an abomination. For this, I should pay for it one way or another and to punish me, my family and this old notable had comploted to poison my husband. As their mission was accomplished by the death of my lover, they went to demonize my family in law, telling them that it was me who was behind the death of my husband. Therefore, me and my innocent children have no right nor to the house or property left by the deceased.

That is my family in law without a criticism spirit was influenced by these sadists. So It was the execution of this decision, they had sent me on the street with my children. After this humiliation, I was forced to leave the village to refuge elsewhere and a widow who was also a victim of the same situation than me welcomed me into her house with a bedroom and living room. Upon arrival, she occupied the living room and she gave us the bedroom. It is with her that I began to raise my children who were still too young. To find something to eat I travelled long distances and worked for almost a week in a significant concession of this village which in turn paid me at the end of days. The weekend I should go to visit my kids. Since seven days of the week, I only had two days where I could stay with my children because the owner of the dealership did not want children to the workplace. The presence of children on the site was an opportunity distraction for his workers.

Once any one who brought the child run the risk of losing his job. My children were also forced to stay with my friend widow who moved almost not seen his age. I took this option to let the kids because I was in front of an accomplish fact. That is to say, keep it keep children starve and let me ensures restoration with all the risk of missing a good education.

Faced to this situation I was thinking on my side facing the first opportunity to ensure their survival and I told myself the rest will take care by the nature. It is in these conditions that your Yaya had grown. As there was not someone who could monitor, each of them as they were all three girls behaved in his way. The result is that my first two of the three found themselves fat. This is the youngest who is your mother, who was married, but unfortunately after your birth, her husband who is your Daddy still running behind his first wife with whom he had divorced before taking your mom to marriage. And as your mom did not want this life of polygamy would lead your Dad, she divorced and they separated.

After your mom home as her two other sisters engrossed or pregnanced, she leaves you in my hands and she decided to start the trade at the side of her cousins who lived in the town that you had been borned. Then, she no longer likes go to live there after the disappointment she had had from your dad. My wish and those of my three children to you, is that you can not tolerate either like me or like them. That's why me and them we are fighting, despite the divorce of your parents, that you grew up in good conditions to acquire wisdom, intelligence and with the help of God and to our ancestors that you become responsible men and useful in the society. That's why I had agreed with them, all three, I tell you that I take in your hand especially education.

So you do not get worried about this divorce because you and your cousins, you're in good hands with your grandmother. And the opportunity to remove them in the existing confusion over the names, saying: I'm not your mom but your grandmother and your Yaya is not your sisters, but your moms. Then i wish you all the best for to prepare your futures. Therefore, despite the shock, ABIBU and his cousins became aware of their situation and they now act with responsability.

TITLE II

THE WAY OF THE SCHOOL

ABIBU is a boy under age six who lived with his grandmother and his cousins in a town along the Congo River. While they lived together, every morning when ABIBU awoke, he found himself alone in the family court. As a child crying was her first reaction and stopped by the assistance from their neighbors. Her grandmother went early in the morning to fetch the source for drinking water and others went to school as they reached school age.

This couldn't enchant our little boy who was struggling to endure isolation every morning when he woke up. As always woke up last of all, he decided one day to opposite, he attended personally done the movement of his grandmother and cousins who were about to go about their business.

It was then that he understood and found resolution, also act the same way every day, to accompany his cousins as a spectator to the river, where they went for their first intimate care. And as this was not enough ABIBU should accompany them to the school where he could not cross the classrooms. Despite his insistence on entering, he found himself once more either alone or accompanied by other people on the way back. For him it was another form of martyrdom which he was exposed. Neighbors who had always lived this theater sought to convince and grandmother and that school officials to enroll the boy.

At the time, in most villages were not yet in kindergarten, but because there was little urgency to exit his unhappy state ABIBU, grandmother and school officials agreed to inscribe small though it had not yet reached the age of first grade. He was about five years old. His registration took place in full school year and this as a free student. The first day he had attended lessons was not only a day of joy as some might imagine, but a hell for him because the pace that he had been seemed strange. He was accustomed to managing his day in his own way, he was forced to do what

11

was required by the teacher and other school officials. Habits in the school who was also a boarding school for religious priests, all student should comply with Catholic morality even if another religion. Where outside of school hours, there were many religious activities were organized. These activities include catechesis, choir, acolytes and others in the premises of the mission.

Being from a Catholic family, ABIBU could be interested in these activities. Besides, he always among the first to present the training sessions or rehearsals to motivate, encourage other students reluctant. Their supervisors or trainers were more older classes, their brothers and lay religious teachers with whom they lived together. The priests did not live in the same mission with them. They had only pastoral turned twice a year to celebrate two great liturgical feasts, commemorating the Nativity of the coming of Jesus Christ and that of Easter which Christians commemorate the death and resurrection of Jesus Christ. The distance between their community to their mission was a hundred miles away.

Hence to achieve the mission should go several hours aboard their motocross. Although there was a priest of the Parish of this mission, but the priests were to turn the occasion, say Masses and other sacraments celebrated. With the arrival of the priest and all the inhabitants of the city reserved him a warm welcome at the entrance to the mission, with greetings from all strata of the population of the place, from chief to subordinate, old men to children, Catholic and non-Catholic.

This could be explained primarily by the fact that he was a white man, because at the time we did not used to seeing a man with white skin. The curiosity and interest in this priest was also due to the fact that he was another person than you could imagine. The prelate was remarkably simple, starting from his attire, his availability and his behavior that some can not believe it. A part of his white cassock, we did not see him with his shirt of the same color and same brand. He spent the whole day surrounded by Christians and non-Christians including children. During his visits to the sick, he made no distinction of religion, and he came to the aid of all the necessities without distinction or condition. This behavior was different from that of our culture, where wearing a suit was repeatedly mocked or sign of suffering or misery. Playing and jocking with the children in our customs was a sign of immaturity and weakness. Make visits to the sick and the elderly especially could result in an exclusion under the pretext of being contaminated, bewitched or cursed.

Hence everyone should take distance and behave according to the habits countered. But with the coming of the priest and his behavior, people began to understand and behave differently while relativizing gradually their taboos and prohibitions. The prelate had become a way of life for this community. In addition to his revolutionary behavior in the sense of doing good, he brought solutions to problems that have been raised by people of all faiths together. This left no one indifferent behavior, which attracted a lot of vocation to the priestly life of young people in this area including ABIBU.

Pushed by the desire to look like this prelate, the young man went up to the catechesis which was considered the first steps to expect the priestly life. Embarked on this adventure while the boy was still a schoolboy, it was not an easy task against other obligations that lay ahead. Before going to school, he should first attend morning Mass and evening after school, he should come to the closing catechesis with visits to the sick. This was for him a way of being in harmony with the demands of his new appointment. With his colleagues catechumens, they learned a lot about their way of being and behaving as future priests and Christians in the long run.

After several months of teaching, training and practice, an assessment test offered them by the prelate himself to sanction and approve the formation of catechumens. He was smart, ABIBU distinguished himself and became a Christian one Easter Sunday in the presence of his family and acquaintances who came to encourage and praise him, because he was in his class who had not been baptized by the fact that they had failed the test posed by the assessment exemplary priest, who by his honesty and uprightness, baptized those who had deserved his decision could not be questioned. Having reached this stage the young man saw his future away and gave a discipline to act with responsibility as a young Christian different from other young people. He adopted a rhythm until the end of primary school where he got a certificate attesting the end of his primary school.

To enter a new cycle ABIBU should be prepared to leave his boarding come to his inclusion in the capital like was the wish of his mother's family. This is to compel his Dad wanted to see his son start minor seminar with the hope of bringing to the priesthood. After negotiation, the desire of his mother's family takes precedence over that of his Father and child joined his family located in the capital.

Upon his arrival, he went to live with his maternal uncle who had his wife and children. The young man could not live with his parents because they were divorced and lived each in his own way. His father was already married to another woman with whom they had children. His mother was unmarried launched commercially where she was traveling at any time. Faced with such a situation of his own parents, his grandmother could not give her grandson in their responsibilities. She chose to entrust the responsibility to his eldest son it was already stable and responsible. Immediately, steps were initiated to find him a good school as his previous institution.

To achieve this it took a lot of sacrifices and energies. Not having enough time, his uncle entrusted in the hands of his brother-in-low who was better placed in this area. They scoured several districts of the capital. The first school chosen was located in the neighboring town to theirs. It belonged to the priests of the Society of Jesuits. An institution in which studying with his cousin who ABIBU shared the same room and accompanied him in his efforts. For its fame and quality of education, the college attracted the attention of many concerned parents of a good education to their children. Unfortunately luck did not smile for our little boy, because he was late for that one stopped with registration for the admission test. Although discouraged, depressed and tired, the group had paid way. They went to another school of Catholic vocation still they managed to enroll in the first year of secondary school. Since the beginning has always been difficult, the young man had also experienced despite everything he had as assets. His first results were not famous, he came close to failure. He was optimistic the second year, he surprises everyone and continued until the end of his life orientation cycle. In addition to his school for his intellectual training, attending ABIBU also under his spiritual training the nearest Catholic Parish in his neighborhood, where he joined the first group of young people under 15 years called Group KIZITO-ANUALITE (KA group) and then after 4 years, he joined the adult group named BILENGE YA MWINDA (light young).

As he wanted to become a priest, he was also involved in organizing recollections by the congregation of priests he had chosen to stay in the consecrated life. This was a way to get acquainted with other senior members of this religious community, while awaiting admission to a degree dependent on state test and evaluation of all the years of training.

Having obtained his BA with ease that he was already intelligent. Given the requirements of that congregation that forced each candidate after graduation to a practical training, by learning the English language considered as the second language of the community and / or professional experience of at least one year. The young man opted for learning english who was also his preference language from the French language was the official language.

This preference was not a random due but he had a taste of his teacher of the first year of secondary school, when he had heard for the first time english. So that the teacher spoke good with good actions, and he had attracted and interest ABIBU, he decided to speak also English as their teacher. Surprised by the condition of the english language as one of the two main languages of the community, even as one of major requirement for admission to the convent only increased the desire among the young boy. Occasionally, he began to search for a good learning center for English language corresponding to the scholarship, with he aim to realize his dream and fulfill the conditions of his congregation. He had finally found a training center near his home town with a frequency of three rotations per week sessions of two hours. Training had a duration of one year, divided into four levels of three months for each level. The transition from one level to another was conditioned by a written and oral test without forgetting the practical work and questions. ABIBU began his first level with colleagues, including a majority of boys and girls a minority.

At the end of the first level, he found that his audience was almost half empty. Several reasons were the basis of this unfortunate situation, some did not have enough money to pay the costs of participation in training and others were discouraged to continue training, or because they failed or they not reflected in the material. This was reflected bitter until the end of his training that he has just finished his two colleagues boys.

Day of each defense had defended his theme that had been proposed by the trainer. In turn, appeared before the ABIBU member jury of four trainers who were taught from the first to the last level, assisted by trained other promotions below. As he was well defended, the jury was selected as an assistant and secretary of the center. The young man took over these functions to any liability eve of his departure for the convent. A separation that left ink and saliva flow to all the staff of the center because it was a big hole and a loss for the center.

It was time for him to integrate the training house and as this community was not in the capital where ABIBU lived, but it was represented by colleagues from another branch of the brothers and sisters of branches sisters from a religious family that branch of priests. The young aspirant was not the only one in this situation. This is what had prompted officials or superiors of the congregation to organize a competition for admission to every corner of the country where were all their candidates. That in accordance with the quota assigned to achieve the desired effective for this promotion. That year, it was the first class where they should admit experimental 15 candidates in total, including 4 in which the capital was ABIBU, 4 in the city where stood the house of formation, two to the mission where the congregation exercised his apostolate and five others in different parts of the country in which candidates postulated by correspondence. For those of the capital, had appointed a native priest who was returning from study abroad, in charge of the promotion of this to organize the test in question. The announcement was made to all candidates who living in the capital to attend a Saturday around 8 o'clock, the Sisters of this religious family for the event.

Arrived that day, the young aspirant brought as agreed; strange thing for him to see that he was found with a score of aspiring candidates contrary to expectations. He does not expect that number because he had never seen any aspiring priest on his way to recollections. Although this surprise was frustrated, but it had not discouraged especially he was sure of himself. A publication of the result ABIBU was the first candidat to get more points.

From where he was admitted with three others who followed him to join the others admitted of other parts of the country. Having taken this step allowed the young aspirants should strive to gather all that they had been asked for travel and training. They should be ready with all this in three months. Fortunately for ABIBU by little job of secretary of the center was already preparing his kit sparing gradually his money in a mutual savings.

With this money, he was able to pay the half of the ticket which was embarrassing for him and he had to meet his other needs related to travel. Day trip travel nuns and a few family members accompanied him to the airport. Just when they should be separate for boarding, anyone of them could not contain the pain of separation. All cry! Two flight hours after they landed and the four young people admitted boarded a minibus of the congregation came to wait at the airport in the city. Said city is considered the third largest city in the country. The priest who came on board this vehicle was the same priest who had examined in the capital and he is their father trainer. He accompanied them to the training house in which they are housed and trained.

At the entrance to the enclosure, they were greeted by other successful candidates who had preceded them. A decent vehicle to their colleagues came retrieve their luggage and put them in a room where were their own. This is local full refurbishment where all newcomers were live. For this, they should not even rest because they found other working and just the time to share, they also began to work.

Soon they turned into masons, painters, carpenters and others, because the community did not foresee another labor than new recruits called propédeutes. Not being used to this pace of work that makes them work wholes, ABIBU and his companions especially the capital struggled to adapt. They could not imagine doing this kind of work in the convent. It was for them a kind of exploitation and slavery they were especially under the direction of a tireless white priest.

Hence a certain disappointment and discouragement born already in their camp. According to them, they believed priority activities for training, such as prayer and study seemed to be neglected in favor of manual work. Two months after the rate had changed a little because they are expected to begin classes in an inter-congregational. It had been relieved and confident for the rest of their training.

Just as they began their training itself with the official opening of the academic year, rebellions also started in the country. It was the time of the disturbances and disorders especially in the province where they were. Various rebel troops overran the eastern region of the country. This complicity with some compatriots who for selfish begin to plunder the resources of the country, killing people, raping women and others. In short, we see a total anarchy and life became difficult.

A morning of the first day of the week for everyone in the city was about to make that everyone in the workplace for employees, the market for buyers and sellers to school students and students, etc.., Bullets crackled around and there was a stampede general. Each took his direction and route, the men in uniform and weapon invade all arteries of the city. Nobody knew neither the source nor the cause of the uprising, but the first was the reflex to save his skin. So many dead and injured there was this day, had panicked the city. It was the announcement and the beginning of the war of aggression of which he is a victim of the country ABIBU.

This war became as normal especially at east of the country where the youth was in religious education. That is to say, people were accustomed to such spectacles events which led to loss of lives and property of people. The bullets pattered to day length. Although it became a habit to wait bullets shot at any time and other evils of war that created some mental psychosis in people who went about more freely to his daily routine. On leaving we had perhaps not the hope of seeing his own in return not to return.

As far as the war was growing, life became increasingly difficult. Young people could no longer communicate with their families. The country started to fall apart, and each prince of war occupied his portion where he reigned supreme. Transactions entered provinces were no longer possible. Travel from one province to another should listen to the head or even the loss of life. ABIBU and his comrades were forced to interrupt their training for a few months in the hope to resume after the cessation of hostilities. But nothing had changed in the opposite situation had worsened and they had to continue their education in this state of mind marked by war.

After this forced family stay just a few of them returned more or for fear of being killed either by lack of means of transport which brought them to their training house. As a result of declining enrollment propédeutes under five in the race, two of whose capital is less ABIBU came. This will cause psychosis abandonment of two of his fellow city whose training house is implemented. His last remaining colleague of the capital with which he had come, he too endured over these events away from his family, especially the announcement several months after the death of his father, a pillar of his family death occurred as a result of that war, he also decided to leave in the middle years of training to get looked after her younger brothers and sisters as an elder of the family.

From his intimate colleague ABIBU also from a family of three children, all boys, only he is the eldest grew into the hands of the family of her divorced mother since childhood, begins to reflect the face of such reality of life. He had neither appetite nor the taste of life. Everything had become sober, sullen, bitter and complicated. His priest trainer and trainer spiritual director had understood the state was formed in the capital he loved the fact that he was the youngest, the nicest and most intelligent of the group in the capital. And not wanting to lose time, he sought ways and means by how to save the situation. He walked more ABIBU while calling him every day not to give or to abandon the competition. Paraphrasing him, he always said to the young: "ABIBU, you have a future ahead of you, but if you do leave you will lose." Whenever the young man awaited these prophetic words, he came to their senses and put aside his feelings and passions.

Thus the young man managed to finish his undergraduate and graduate its first stage of training. While waiting with his two colleagues with whom they have finished the first stage of religious life, a confirmation step is a key intellectual for further training in religious life, the three winners in anticipation of their snack academic and ecclesiastical focus remained in their home training. A day in the middle of the week since ABIBU after washing laundry and wanting to make a right turn at the Institute to accompany his colleagues promotions below the lists were not displayed, they heard again bullets crackled.

That time it was accompanied balls shelling with heavy weapons. All understood that it was serious, the unusual, the unexpected. At the moment they came to the military positionnèrent gradually and people sought each place of refuge. As the winner and his companions were a few meters from their community and to save their skins, because the gate was closed and the feeling had also taken the beam escampette, they decided to violate the rules of procedure of the congregation by retracting their closure. Once inside, they realized that their colleagues wholes were not in the pen. Although they were concerned about the absence of their colleagues, within the scope of the bullets striking the first priority was to get everyone in the room to hide and see the rest later. This statement came from their trainer who came to join them, after he had also escaped death in his race with the vehicle was out.

Saw what had lived in the city where he came from, the Superior father priest had no solutions other than those educated applicants. He advised everyone while he was in his room to concentrate in prayer. And asked all workers who were already in the confines of the community to return home lest he die by bullets along the way. For this reason, he forced them to occupy two rooms including one for all men and another for all the other women. As for himself, he went to take refuge in the chapel confided in God. The first day ended in a state of constant crackling balls. Later in the night, the Father Superior community manager left the chapel where he was praying to visit his flock, the time for him to visit and make sure if everyone was healthy. He visited his foremost and trained workers.

During his tour, they brought a few bottles of sweet drinks and a few packets of biscuits that were in the store, so they use it as a provision because he already sensed that this war would take several days. With this visit was all starting comforted by the priest himself to the applicants including workers. They slept and woke up the next day in a state of war. On the third day they lost their livestock due to the death of all the ports in a series that fell within the confines of the barn. The loss shocked them all, but they were powerless against this high tragedy because even they themselves lived in a total uncertainty. They said anything could happen to any of them and it anytime. On the occasion they decided to stay together as follows: a first chamber for all applicants, the second for the priest, the third for working moms and one for male workers. This decision was taken to overcome the fear that lived in each of them and consolidate the hope that they began to lose slowly. They stayed until the seventh day, when the soldiers of one of two groups that had come face to dislodge the four rooms where they are refugees.

Although they had but the provision did not eat, because nobody had appetite. Recover before the military and their provision because they do not clearly understand their identities, they brought them all under the command of chief place in a large plot in the form of a villa. This residence was owned by a notable city which had become the headquarters of this group of soldiers. On the way to the residence hostages saw several corpses who fell in their presence and others who are already broken.

As they went into the Headquarters under the command of the highest ranking of all the military, accompanied by two soldiers, one of which was in front and the other behind, they were educated in their follow every movement of the soldier who was at the forefront lest they die easily and unnecessarily before the judgment that awaited them in the villa. This order was given by the official result of the interrogation that he had submitted to the priest of the Congregation of higher ABIBU. As they emerged from the pen of their community as they had been found. They closed their rooms and left everything except their rosaries and crosslets. They followed to the letter the instructions and they came into the headquarters, with one hand and slippers others without slippers.

Arrival there, they were sitting on the ground by force under the command of the commander of the rebel group. He once again submit to a second examination that would determine their fate be to live or die on the spot. This was not a joke or a joke because they had seen with their own eyes, how they took away the lives of the people themselves qualifiaient suspects. Good shooters arms around them and waiting for the watchword of their leader to spend at runtime. As their supreme leader was in communication with the officer who had transferred to him, he again submitted the priest a long examination of more than two hours. Fortunately, the Lord had filled the prelate of incredible wisdom and had touched the heart of this senior official to believe the words of the priest.

After having listened to the supreme commander ordered the soldiers to accompany the subordinate priest and all his group to the parish where the caller had suggested for their safety. They left the residence and went to the parish of refuge along these soldiers. When they arrived at the church, Christians saw the host in tears because they did not expect to see their spiritual fathers in these conditions. At the moment each of them ran home and brought back to what gave the priest and his retinue. As parish priest was not enough space to accommodate guests, he constructed with the help of two local parishioners can accommodate survivors. Already in the evening the father superior had found it expedient to release wholes workers so that everyone regains its respective families. He remained with his trainers.

Although communication was a problem at that time because there was not yet mobile cellular devices, the priest with his had received grants, to send information to the appropriate authorities. Despite these efforts, the high authorities of church had difficult to join them to assist them materially. Meanwhile, they had to settle for contraient this miserable situation in which they crossed. Two weeks after they finally receive assistance from the parent of the congregation. Assistance in cash and kind that was really relieved and allowed to recover some lost property. They returned to their community devastated and plundered by the men in uniform. They only recover some documents but the rest was carried away by the attackers.

As their community was besieged by the soldiers, in addition to the loss of their plunder and should be added dirt that filled it. Arrival there, they began to be essential while putting some order in their house training provided it becomes habitable. According to the rules that governed the congregation, the next step after the training they had finished, should be done in another country than yours. Thus, despite the state of war which they were subjected, and the three young finalists should continue to preparative because he only had two weeks. It was a difficult time for ABIBU mainly because he could not communicate with his family who had remained in the capital. His other two brothers were able to see and speak with their own. But it was not the young formed of the capital because the masters of war each had a portion of the country they ruled supreme. The country was divided into several fractions each occupied by a warlord and his cronies.

After transcending this suffering ABIBU and his two colleagues began the steps of the journey. Despite all these difficulties, they eventually meet in two weeks all training. Thus came the stage of the journey itself, to find a plane that can move to the city where they were for this country.

The planes were landing at the airport and often the few who landed were those of soldiers from two neighboring countries allied to the two rebel groups that existed in the province. As there was still no planes as they approached the deadline for the start of the training, they were forced to negotiate the space in these cargo planes military. They came to convince the rebels and they traveled the night aboard a cargo plane that had no seat for sitting. They stood up by hanging files throughout the trip. They landed very late at night.

This delay put them in a situation much more difficult because they do not know that city. Luckily they were found in the hands of the kind policeman that guided the airport to the hotel where they had been told to go at night. When they came to the reception, they say that there were no rooms available for three people. For this, they should go elsewhere, another equation in front of them. They tried to explain their situation to the receptionist, but without success. At the exit of the hotel under the pressure officers guard the hotel, they decided to entrust the policeman they had met outside. This in contrast to the fear and despair they had against him, according to their grievances attended by carers to the hotel that could accommodate them. They thanked him sincerely and wanting to give him a little money in recognition, the policeman flatly refused. By cons, they say, "it is not important to give me money because I have help you, because I have done only my job as a police officer is to make you safe, keep your money for other needs, especially as you still have a long way to go, you sit so well for the continuation of your trip tomorrow with any force." At these words, the police withdrew to join his fast workstation.

This reaction surprising three foreigners because they have never seen such a man in uniform in their country of origin behave this way. They praised their God for having sent a man they considered an angel and intercede for his blessing. The next morning, they wake up quickly ran to the place where they had met him just to show him once again thank them, but they found him more, instead they met another police officer. Trying to find out if he was still there, they answer that he was already gone home for family rest and he will be back the next day. They regretted shortly returned to the hotel and all sad.

As they knew they were leaving the hotel no later than noon, they took advantage to shop and visit the city this country. After they packed their bags, they went to the parking lot to find a bus that should accompany them into the town where their new house of formation. The city to which they had landed yesterday night it was the capital of the country and where they went was the second city of the country. They paid their tickets and boarded the bus. They traveled nearly eight hours to reach that city.

Arrived in this city, they took a taxi which took them up in front of their community. When the driver rang bed, they saw the sentry come open the door. After giving informed of the new brothers of the community, he went also inform the superior of the community who came quickly greet with other colleagues. They led directly into the chapel to give thanks to God because they were already desperate for everything they had learned from them about the war.

The output of the chapel, they went all the refectory for supper. They spent an evening community atmosphere. In this atmosphere they began their training until the day ABIBU decided himself to leave this life for personal reasons.

TITLE III

THE VACATIONER

The geo-cosmological realities of ABIBU country had an impact on the daily life in general and the school calendar in particular until these days. During a school year or even academic, school children and students receive three types of holiday: Christmas, Easter and major holidays. The first two holidays each take about two weeks and two months for major holidays. The first two did not attract any of the young man in his projected journey, but unless they had a specific character for him as a Catholic Christian. Because it is during these two holiday religious affiliation famous nativity, death and resurrection of Jesus Christ it sees as Lord and Savior.

To this end, each parish is actively preparing to welcome tourists by organizing several parish activities. This in order to attract the largest number of students especially, middle and high school. They passed most of their holidays in the parish, sometimes to participate in various spiritual exercises and the various games organized in church groups and service management. Among these groups we include choirs, acolytes group, the group of young light, the group Xavier, the Scot, the group KA (Kizito-Anuarite) and others.

The atmosphere in the parish of ABIBU could only be attracted to the more permanent church elsewhere. But during the major holidays, another reality is on the horizon. A large majority of students prefer to leave the familiar surroundings. They went from one end to the other while priming the minimum necessary given the length of stay. Transport is not easy to ABIBU country. Holidaymakers should wait several days to reach their holiday destinations.

This due to the dilapidated condition of road communication, the mishandling of carriers and their gear and harassment by various departments of the State. All this left no one indifferent and all was often moved with pity upon arrival. In regards ABIBU often the only means of transport for him, it was the boat. To access a lengthy procedure was initiated. It should start by doing book a place by paying the tickets to the locations indicated. Once in possession of a ticket, it would occasionally go to the port to make sure the day of departure, repeatedly postponed for various reasons or organizational and other sentimental. When the day of departure was confirmed, it is not required for all passengers to report to the port the day before to make everyone aware of his place and spend the night. Those who had a lot of baggage and cargo, he had been recommended to load some before departure. ABIBU and his three companions left early in the morning to head to the port.

Despite being one of the first arrival, but will be shipped from the past because they did not know the members of the crew or with agents assigned to the service, which gave priority before all their friends and knowledge. Even if it had not pleased, they were forced to accept this reality as such. To early morning departure, while sleeping in it, the captain and his crew are set to work to leave the boat at the port to the deep waters of the river. In the boat, there were different classes ranging from first class to third class. The first was reserved for wealthy individuals or VIP. The second to the middle class and the last to the lower class does not have enough means.

This boat was destined for the country's third largest city, which was also the last navigable point of the river. Other cities and centers of the country were considered only as boat docking stations for just a few hours to allow passengers to disembark called to release the boat to give up their seats to passengers and other new opportunity for those who are to be supplied. Usually the normal travel time from the place of embarkation to destination was two weeks. But this time they had reached two weeks before the destination due to the decrease of the river due to low water period of the dry season. ABIBU and his companions landed the boat and then join the village of their parents was right on and along the river. They will be welcomed by those princes in the village. This gesture comforted feasibility and forget all the sufferings of the trip.

A week after having observed the movements and activities of its cousins in the village, ABIBU also decided not to remain only an observer. His wish was to participate in one way or another in all activities. Evening around the fire family, he spoke and said every time when you go in the morning to your daily activities, you never think interest us to accompany you. This has never settled, that's why I expressed my dissatisfaction, because I need also to learn how to clear the field, how to fish, how to hunt and others. Immediately reactions come from all sides saying that this kind of work was not for city dwellers, but to them. No, replied the young urban energy: "It is a great mistake to think so because in life we have lot of surprises. Today we are citizens, we can become tomorrow as villagers and vice versa. Being a citizen is neither a privilege nor an excuse, we are all equal because we are all human beings created in the image of God with all the same rights and duties." His argument convince his interlocutors. In the morning the head of the family ordered that the instrument makes fishing so that he will also fishing with other boys of the village.

Since ABIBU interest and participate in daily activities of the village, his brothers with whom they came mocked him. These jokes did not change his ambitions, instead it encouraged him to persevere. After several tries, he gradually adapted to this life and learned some techniques to plow the land, fish and hunt. Having found his determination to learn their business, his brothers-in-low invited him one day to accompany the fishing was done in the canoe on the river with nets.

This fishery use to be done at distant islands to hope catching more fish. Insteade to be discouraged the citizer young gladly accepted the invitation. The whole night they prepared to fishing and the early hours of the following day they went to this place for their task. In return they brought a lot of fish with what they sold part and the other part of it is served for restoration.

From that day, ABIBU advised that whenever he could come back fishing with fish if he could kept in smoked or salted fish. At the end of his vacation, he managed to gather a lot of fish crammed into a traditional basket made by the villagers who had enjoyed and loved by his curiosity and simplicity mostly remarkable. On this occasion, they offered him several gifts. All these packages received from his own efforts and gifts of his relatives had helped prepare his new school unlike his cousins who had returned almost hand reduced. This was more delighted his grandmother who hosters in the capital.

Consequently, the holidays were no longer just a tourist trip but productive. Therefore, the ABIBU prepared with all possible seriousness, purchasing necessary according to the needs recommended by the specialists themselves fishing, hunting and field. This approach was used as an example to his other brothers and sisters who finally nested its not so little as to contribute to their own growth and education.

The trip to his parents' village had become a habit for ABIBU during major holidays. Among his favorite activities included fishing as their preference. That day as usual the citizer young woke to the early hours of that day to go fishing with his brother-in-low while he was still night. They left the village first of a canoe in which were all necessary for fishing. After a few hours of travel on the river, they arrived at the designated area and began fishing. They caught a lot of fish. That day to the afternoon they noticed a small change in climate, but it had at all worried. They continued peacefully and simply go about their occupation.

Shortly after violating the wind surprise while they were in action. The wind caused large waves, the river and the sky shook so black. Lack of experience and mastery ABIBU cried for help, weeping orally because this was the end of the world. His brother-in-low instead urged him to keep his composure and not panic. Accustomed to such, he then says that there was no question of despair, but take courage to face this ordeal.

As the situation was only getting worse, the brother-in –low ordered ABIBU no longer continue to paddle that he should take care of the boy and that should take care to pour the water from the boat. Because it did not work, the brother-in-low will use another solution, which to be flowing into the water and let the boat empty but cling to it.

This will allow them to finally reach the shore without losing the boat and all its contents. Having reached the shore, the young man saw himself in heaven, because for him it was a miracle to face of such extraordinary wave had caught the full middle of the river. Immediately the tears had changed to joy. His brother-in-low congratulated for having more observed his instructions during the test. As for himself, he congratulated himself for having faced a great test of his life. Since that day he felt really been a man. And fear disappear in his life because he said he was prepared for any eventuality in life. Return from his holiday in the capital everyone noticed the great change of behavior in the person of ABIBU.

SECTION II

THE SECOND STEP

TITLE IV

THE TALK

How shameful realities, disappointing, unhappy that his country traversed the country in general and its particular city, which was the capital of the country where the bad outweighed the good, the greatest concern ABIBU level. To fight his way to his antivalues invading all layers of the population, the young man decided to go to the meeting of all those involved in this crisis. The way in which he could win his bet was the dialogue. Thus he solves not let an opportunity at every opportunity that presented itself to him, despite all risk potential in this approach.

One day when he awoke to begin his apostolate, he approached his parents that his parents were going to go about their daily business. Apologetically, he said, dear parents, I know this will surprise you certainly because I want to talk to you about something that concerns me at the moment. This concern comes down to these questions:

- Dear parents, what makes some parents often fail to take their responsibilities to their children?

Speaking in his capacity as head of the family, dad react: dear son, would not it be interesting to postpone the meeting in the evening? All happy, respectful young man agreed and proposed to his father to chain once and for all with another question that remained. Go quickly, his father said, as long as it does not take enough time!

Then the young boy continued his interrogation.

- Why, some parents who opted to join the wedding, a means by which we can continue the divine work of procreation, they do not wish this to heart moved before men and before?

Your questions seem interesting and relevant, but appointment tonight, said the father with the consent of his wife at his side and they parted with these words. The evening came, ABIBU showed up the first and the last speakers arrived. The serious stuff began.

Dad attended his wife speaks, responds to his son: "I and thy mother, thy wise men were surprised by the questions in the morning. You know, it could surprise us too, because we know that you were always with intelligence and extraordinary wisdom. In our capacity as parents, your questions concern us directly and indirectly. Because we are directly involved as parents and indirectly because we are not that kind of parents who you alluded to in your response. That is to say, those who do not take care of their children for one reason or another. This irresponsibility is subject to several factors:

- From the political point of view: there is not a good wage policy in the country. The wages paid to workers here, does not allow parents to take care of their homes.

- From an economic standpoint: the purchasing power of household or basket of the population is too low. This does not allow that one to cover the end of the month. As a result, it uses the principle that every man for himself and God for all.

- From the social point of view: with the crisis in the country, unemployment is at its record. Some malignant advantage of this situation, create the churches to operate their own and sleep down people in the name of the gospel. Faithful followers or victims of exploitation or believe they can solve find succeed to their problem with these churches. One of the solutions provided by these pastors or shepherds would get rid of witches, who in most cases are the children of a stepmother or other family members as his.

Faced with this unfortunate situation, said the father, parents are often faced the complication situation, despite the desire can be theirs eventually break. This situation is far from being settled by a lack of leadership and popular will to change things. These explanations are clear and explicit, pushed interlocutors to finish the interview. Speaking, he said thank you very much for giving me daddy clarification regarding my concerns.

But to hear you speak, I felt you in despair. That is to say that you do not give no chance for our country. Non Dad, i think we must be optimist face to that situation, may we have conscious and react in a another way in order to change things.

About the international community

One day while ABIBU was on the street race for his boss, he sees a car park with the words of the United Nations "UN", a group of four white foreigners, down from the vehicle, dressed in military uniforms other than their soldiers. They entered a large supermarket where was the young man. They dispersed each in his corner for shopping with baskets in hand. One of them got the radius where the boy was, not knowing too the realities of place, he turned to him with a question of accuracy with respect to items he needed and he will answer given by the young man and he did not hesitate to thank.

Curious about the right way shown by this stranger ABIBU got the opportunity to interact with the host, who seemed to be surprised by the interest that he gave his new partner already asked his first question: Excuse me sir, although not be prepared for such a surprise but please transcend your limits, to satisfy myself as to my turn to these questions I intend to ask me to go a clear relation to these realities.

- What did we do to the international community that we experience today all kinds of injustice?

- Why can not we enjoy the outrageous wealth of the soil and subsoil like many other countries, independent and sovereign?

- Do you think the international community honestly work for us? or rather it came to his own interests?

My dear friend, said his new partner: remember this in your life that "there is nothing for nothing in life." While the international community is represented by an institution called: united nations, whose mission is to support the countries of the world to maintain good relations. It does not assume the role of referee as it should. Proof as you ask well the question, we are a potentially rich and outrageous. In principle, as an independent and sovereign country, we should fully enjoy our independence and our sovereignty to benefit from our wealth.

Alas, this is not the case for multiple reason I want to try with you according to my own analysis: your wealth attracted the enthusiasm of the great powers of the world, which are countries that have the monopoly of this institution by that they largely fund said organization. This fund is done through various interventions to the problems posed by these countries. That is to say rich countries often come in aid to poor countries like your.

These countries believe that supporting others, do not just in the name of solidarity with others, but they have other intentions than to dominate and further exploitation. These are the same countries benefactors, taking advantage of the naivety of your leaders, causing wars and unrest in poor countries said that they reach their goals. It is in these conditions they were able to plan their dehumanizing, because they do not put on the center of their action the people, but rather their own selfish interests.

About the authorities of the country

ABIBU spoke to his father about the country's authorities.

- Why our authorities act in most cases as if this country did not belong to them, leaving it to sink into the dark, or they are able by their studies and expertise, to make our country a paradise?

- Why should they not overcome their differences and interests and partisan interests to pull the country out of this crisis, which dates back many years and we distancias further development and any consideration?

- Why change as expected and desired by the people delayed, and the standard of living of the population remains very low, while it is sitting on a floor and a basement very rich?

Speaking, the father responds: "My son, these authorities we often are imposed by the international community. As it is so, their choice in most cases does not meet the choose of the population. They choose our authorities according to their own criteria and in line with their interests. Why they prefer non-nationalistic instead of nationalists who may be concerned about their country and their people. Those where they are serving their Western sponsors that population. That is to say, they first obey the orders given by the Western imperialists, lest they lose their jobs or be totally lost their lives.

Our country is under Western domination, nothing can happen without his consent. Everything is decided there and we do suffer. Although today there is an awakening of patriotic population begins to announce here and there to give our country leaders need because we are not the only country affected by this injustice, but the steps to be much. This is not a cause for discouragement, rather an exhortation to each of us to become aware of our situation so that together we went to this slavery.

About the political opponent.

ABIBU spoke to his father saying:

- Why, those who call themselves opponents against which constitute a burden for leaders in office, do not often direct their actions in the common interest of the people?

- Why, opponents often have difficult to speak the same language as they claim to defend the people against the bad governance of those who lead us?

Replicating, the father said: "My son, know that in our country that we did not have real opponents because they see first and foremost their interests, even if they pretend to speak in the name of the people, their actions are often referred to their own interests. They do not make at heart the suffering of the population. They act primarily for their own interests to the detriment of the whole people, which has also the responsibility to help our political class towards a new vision of patriotism. This is the way where each of us can make a building block to our beloved and beautiful country, dive in a crisis desired by us who live it.

About men of God.

ABIBU turned to his father and said:

- Why our men of God who are supposed to receive from the Lord the mission of preaching the Good News to the people, so that it shows through this gospel acts, do not perform as it should be?

- Why the Church of God is not united as was once the case with the early Christians, who served as good examples to the present day through their stories of life?

- Why, these men of God do not teach to the faithful the true love, the way by which the country could hope for a lasting peace that leads to development?

In response, the father replied: my son know well that in that field there are drink and food. Most of these men of God you see, they are not by vocation. There are true men of God who became by vocation and those who have become by accident. That is to say, those who have become for any reason or a specific purpose. This is due today through there are several deviations from these men. But Christians as we are also, have the responsibility to help them to lead well God's children.

About teachers.

ABIBU spoke to his father, saying:

- Why teachers who are expected to pass through their teaching methodologies and tactics, knowledge to students, the elite of tomorrow, do not make them like they should be?

- Why do not they provide a quality education today as was once the case with previous generations?

- Why, studies in these days in our country have lost their special place in the lives of our youth, when everyone knows the importance of education?

In response the father responds: if we live such of situation where our teachers can not produce a quality education as previously was formerly the case, and this independently and depending on their wishes. Regardless of their intentions, because education has become an area of mockery. The fact that they are not well paid. To survive, they indulge in corruption and all sorts of impunity. They no longer have enough time to devote to research and preparations of their subjects.

Wholes without the means and conditions necessary to work well, they just small ways to make the most edge in their business. Although there are efforts being made by some teachers to raise the level of education in our country, but there is not a good educational policy and a willingness on the part of our leaders to promote education, the finding remains bitter.

About businessmen

ABIBU spoke to his father and said:

- Why these businessmen who are well positioned financially and physically can not get involved in helping the country out of this crisis?

- Why do they use their wealth and assets to exploit and abuse their own people poor, sometimes painful and hard work, they became what they are today?

- Why do they prefer to invest elsewhere than in our country, a way to encourage and support the nation so little development?

The father reacts by saying: the business climate in our country does not allow our serious businessmen to invest in our country. They are not themselves security including their investments by our justice. The few businessmen who dare to do something, they have done with risk and perish. That is to say, at any time and the opportunity to nothing, just switch and lose everything that you can have in one way or another. This worrisome situation does not allow businessmen to trust on our country.

About expatriates

ABIBU turned to his father and said:

- Why, expatriates who have chosen our country as their second home, which makes them residents by the hospitality of its citizens, we are not grateful for their behaviors?

- Why do not they respect in most cases, populated full of goodness, who wanted to live with them, despite the treatment they are often the victims when they go to their country of origin?

- Why, these expatriates often go against the laws established in our country?

Reacted, the father said, you see expats settle in our country, some among them, are illegally. Most are in hiding or without documents or with false documents. Arrived here on site, they make friends with our civilian and military authorities, who support them whenever they commit crimes. With this support, they can mistreat our population, either by forced labor with low wages, or by various indifference and injustice. They become untouchables, privileged, rights holders and other part of the wealthy class.

About popular musicians

ABIBU asked and said to his father:

- Why, popular musicians who believe they have received the gift of educating people through their songs, can not use their talents for this purpose?

- Why do they take the nonsense above through their works and performances, while morality should accompany their works?

- Why, the love theme in the pejorative sense is on the top of other themes, while other themes to exploit are numerous and they often use obscene dances?

In response the father said: most of our popular musicians that you see do not have a good character. These are young people who do not like any of the studies. They spent all their time on the street by going to talk about nonsense, or to discuss the lives of politicians, musicians, athletes, comedians, brief stars. In the street, they have access to education diffuse. Rare are those who reach the level of baccalaureate and those who achieve it is through illegal means. Faced with such a category of people, it is impossible to think a certain morality in what they do or what they produce such works.

Being limited, they think the only way to sell their goods, is the love of singing in the pejorative sense with nonsense including obscene dances. They do not have enough sense of initiative, they prefer or simply copying what already exists as long as they make money. Unaware of their role in society, education and awareness of the population is not their concern. The main thing for them is to be popular and famous even in evil, the rest does not concern them.

About Christian musicians

ABIBU spoke to his father by saying:

- Why the Christian musicians who are supposed to convey the divine message through their songs with the aim to convert and change the hearts of those who listen to them, do not really focus for this cause?

- Why do not they use examples or models as expressed in their songs, as people expect them this testimony of life, which differentiate them from other categories of musicians?

- Why, their compositions are often not oriented to persuade and edify the people of God who never ceases to encourage and support them?

Speaking, the father responds:

These musicians are primarily Christian citizens like so many others, each with feelings. Although they are called Christian musicians share the orientation of their works, but often their behavior does not fit this category of people. Initially, most of them were not prepared for this career life, they have become by chance, by accident. There are those who would not even contemplate and have never been trained for such of a career. Another reality is that a person who knows how to sing but he did not receive this divine gift by his behavior and testimony as a model for others. These are the observations which he has always contradiction between what sings a Christian musician and what he himself lives.

About the Military

ABIBU turned to his father and said:

- Why the military who are supposed to defend the nation face to the invasion of any external threat, it does not execute as it should be, then they take an oath to the flag for this case?

- Why they are willing to see the blood of our people run every day as if he had not an army that could defend them?

- Why, the population has become an object of molestation and other forms of violence or threats, while their mission is to watch over the latter?

The father replied:

These soldiers that you see are not well trained. Moreover, the recruitment criteria of our military are almost non-existent, even a criminal can be provided as desired. It is enough to be physically fit so that we become morally military is not. How we become dependent on military affinities or relationships that you can have with a civil or military authorities. That is to say, we may or may not be formed, but become a soldier. Once in the service it is believed to be above and beyond any law. They justify their harassment made to the people by the fact that they are underpaid. To overcome this situation, they use people to meet their needs.

About policemen

ABIBU turned to his father and said:

- Policemen by the role assigned to them to protect and secure the population and their property, they do not perform as it should be?

- Why do not they try to earn the trust of that population who treats today vandalistes, protagonists instead of partners?

- Why do we record today for theft, rape and murder of almost everywhere throughout the country, while there are security capable in this regard?

The father responds by saying:

The same fact applied to the military can be applied to the policeman, the fact that they are all birds of a feather. They are starting out groups of offenders, who decide immoral or lack or to either prove or retaliate against an antecedent, it is enlisted in the service ordered. Thus all his actions will be directed to all sorts of crimes or abuse of the population. They are the first in their ignorance to create disorder, as they are called law enforcement officers. Their attitude becomes even worse by the fact that they are not well paid. Therefore it is the people who must pay the broken pot.

At this stage, it is difficult to trust on our men in uniform. Especially during events, they become more and more furious faced the population and they do not hesitate fired point blank at the protesters, then they forget that these claims concern them too.

About the doctors and nurses

ABIBU spoke to his father and said:

- Why, doctors and other medical bodies have taken the Hippocratic oath to care for the sick, they do not act according to this oath?

- Why do they leave the hospital bed patients to their fate, focusing primarily money and their own interests?

- Why do not they occur first for the person suffering, knowing that human life or health has no price?

Speaking, the father said:

Wholes doctors and other medical bodies like any other fellow in our country are motivated by bad faith. Our love is bound by interest, because of the property, we are willing to sacrifice the lives of others, even those who call themselves believers always behave the same way. Faced with a difficult situation, we abandon the friend to his own fate and a fortiori that the person no connection or knowledge, it will be crazy. It is in this way that the dead see all around us, the victims of this unfortunate and irresponsible behavior.

About sportmen

ABIBU turned to his father and said:

- Why athletes who are able, through their various disciplines, to generate revenue and foreign exchange as other state services, and make them useful men in society, they are not up to their task?

- Why are they doing now their disciplines a way to delinquency, disrupting public order through unnecessary disturbances they cause in the streets?

- Why they are today characterized and identified by the vandalism that makes them men to take with great caution for fear of being a victim of threats and other abuse?

Speaking the father responds:

Athletes that you see through, are also classified in the same category as our military and police in general, not having a good framework or a good base from their parents. Once they have bissepses with bulging bellies, they believe themselves to be strong men and daunting. Knowing no theoretical concept compared to their respective disciplines and facing an almost non-existent, they engage in acts of vandalism. This approach gives them bread, because by doing so, they feel much more comfortable.

About the Media men

ABIBU, addressed to his father, saying:

- Why, the media people who are supposed to inform and educate the population by their noble and loyal profession, do not fulfill properly their professional duties?

- Why, this mission is now diverted to the moral depravity that fact that today in our families, the parents can not stay together with their children to follow their programs on radio and television for fear that 'they are the easy or outraged?

- Why, they get carried away by both styles of stars, our politicians and many other guests for their trays, they are losing their identity?

Speaking, the father responds by saying:

Media men commonly called journalists are also victims of the governance of our country, by their training even in their workplaces. Besides all these television channels and radio stations in which working men of feathers, each have a membership or political, social and ideological, that they are subject to comply. If not obedience, discipline is in follow up licensement. On the one hand they are subject to this regulation and on the other side they are also stubborn to labor issues, which do not allow them to do their work.

Faced with such truth, they prefer to put it another way is to please his superiors or their guests. This is to gain the trust of the boss or is expected to have something from his guest.

Once consciousness is corrupted everything is sloppy and nothing good is expected. We do not know even consider professional ethics.

About tradesmen

ABIBU turns to his father and said:

- Why tradesmen who have agreed to serve the people through their various trades such as tailors, shoemakers, carpenters and others, do not make them like they should be?

- Why, they use their trades today to cause harm to the population, by false promises, deceit, lies and other immoral behavior?

- Why, they often abuse the trust that the public has always placed by presenting them, despite this uncertainty, their property réfectionner or repair?

Speaking, the father responds:

Tradesmen you see, it is this class of people who have created their small companies with a limited number of students they supervise or be a small number of workers they hired. Generally, these are people who live daily receipts. Faced with this situation, it is rare to see someone in these fields let a customer in his eyes, even if he is busy with other work, he prefers it without realizing cluttered work he expects. This is what makes the day of the appointment, they fail to honor their promises. Therefore they end up creating problems with customers who treat less serious.

Laurent Lokwa Tshimbeka

About the intellectuals

ABIBU spoke to his father and said:

- Why, intellectuals who are regarded as the pillar and the lifeblood of our country, through their thoughts and guidance, does not involve too much for this cause?

- Why do they let themselves engulfed by the common mortal, who now leads the country in total drift and whose consequences are already on the entire nation?

- Why are they leave and get discouraged to promote the role of the elite Congolese society that is still looking for its development?

Speaking, the father responds:

Intellectuals that we are now ignored by our leaders and the general population. As most of them are civil servants, poorly paid, they no longer have a say in the illiterate. This category of the population, which once was a class of pride and a model for other classes, became an object of ridicule. They no longer serve as a model for the current generation, who instead of spending student prefers business to make money quickly, to position in life. Studies for them became not only an object of mockery but also a way that leads to poverty. This situation discourages intellectual traps and to move forward.

About men of law

ABIBU turned to his father and said:

- Why, men of law have a duty to render justice to the people without discrimination of class, race, tribe, gender and other social classes do not as it should be?

- Why they are not involved in the strict application of the law without discrimination to build a rule of law that protects and guarantees the rights and duties of citizens?

- Why, injustice reigns it absolute master at the expense of justice is stifled, their personal interests and supporters?

Speaking the father responds:

In a country such as ours, it is difficult that we have right honest men. Irrespective of their own volition because they are time constraints beyond their understanding. They are forcing their leaders who, for one reason or another, to decide a case in favor of those who most influential or more frica even if he has committed a crime or an offense that merits a repair or even a exemplary punishment and severe. In this world, it is the law of the strongest prevails over the other. A poor has never been right and the rich always been victorious. The men of law in this country have never been free before their consciences. They act not in the name of justice, but rather in the name of money. Every time they dare to do justice, they are victims of threats that may harm their work or even their physical integrity with risk of losing his own life, including his family. Therefore, it should remain in the same logic to satisfy the rights holders and wealthy.

About State officials

ABIBU turned to his father and said:

- Why, officials of the State to which the administration of the country has been entrusted to develop all sectors, for a job well done on their part, do not like it should?

- Why, he now reigns anarchy in their different services or everyone can do anything, which destroyed more this area?

- Why do not they serve as an example to other employees working in the private sector to change the image of our workers, this to attract donors to invest more in the country?

Speaking, the father responds:

The state officials you see are primarily responsible families. Today they are also victims of poor stewardship of our country. Our leaders share the spoils between them without considering other officials centerpieces. Following their salary arrears of more than ten months, they languish in extreme poverty. Find even transportation to their place of service is a stunt. Others prefer the foot to avoid any kind of humiliation. How do you want someone who works in such circumstances can give a good performance?

To overcome this situation some of them prefer to stay at home and go do something else or at the end of the month in the hope of hitting the crumbs of salary. Others who dare to go to work, use downright office supplies to resolve itself so little to their needs.

About the diaspora

ABIBU spoke to his father and said:

- Why our compatriots who opted to leave the country to live other countries for various reasons, do not they think the fate of their countries stagnate in misery?

- Why they do not participate actively in the development of their country as do other citizens of friendly countries?

- Why, the reputation of our diaspora often unsatisfactory, a behavior that does not honor our country?

Speaking, the father responds:

Our compatriots living abroad were not easily installed in its host countries as at home here. They live in difficult conditions. They are subject to works that do not honor them, but because they are forced to live, they accept them despite doing these types of work, through which they are able to pay for their education, their housing, their restorations and especially other charges in the country.

About Carrier men

ABIBU turned to his father and said:

- Why, carrier men who use the roadways and river and air to facilitate the movement of people and deliver goods to their destinations, they not realize this mission seriously?

- Why, they often tend to sail, ride and fly without reservation, without measuring risks and consequences of loss of life and material goods?

- Why, their behavior often inadequate for non-compliance with codes road, river and air and even your customers with insolent words with molestation?

Speaking, the father responds:

Our carrier men are people who do not care about time of their lives. They do not care about anything, especially when they roll the wheel to the vehicle drivers. They forget that they are human beings, not aliens, much less spam; accident that think they may be exempted. This is a serious error on the part of the drivers, who instead of driving the craft well distracted in futility. This behavior is often in collusion with the police station, which lets these uncivil after corrupted by them. As they know they are supported in their nonsense, they can do anything. This situation creates uncertainty among travelers. The trip became a reason for fear and fear for those who travel. Upon arrival to the destination, they praise and glorify God for having arrived without incident.

About trader men

ABIBU spoke to his father and said:

- Why trader men whose activities lucrative for their survival and that of the nation, do not make a conscious?

- Why they do not pay their taxes properly to the public treasury, for that money, in turn, allows the State to fill up its obligations?

- Why, they often tend to exaggerate the pricing of their products and services, forgetting the interests of the population who is like their partner?

Speaking, the father responds:

Trader men generally are people who always tend to raise prices of their products, they benefit from a nothing to make big profits. Given the disarray in our country, traders instead of paying taxes properly, they prefer to negotiate these charges with the agents at discounted prices, which in turn employ money for their own end. In doing so, they make more money illegally. These are people who do not wish to see this country move towards a change. They know that one day when this country became a constitutional state where everything is in order, their activities fall into bankruptcy. They increase both their goods due to numerous harassments against them during the course of their activities and other difficulties in transporting their products.

About owners of compound.

ABIBU turned to his father and said:

- Why, owners of compounds and owners of concessions which lease their plots to third parties or to dwell in gainful employment, often behave in inhuman?

- Why do not they see their partners as tenants as citizens with rights and duties, instead they often make life difficult?

- Why, tenants are often victims of exaggeration or guarantees prices for rent rental, or even, fraud for their own selfish needs?

Speaking, the father responds:

My son, donors who rent their homes to third parties for one reason or another, are doing so because they are primarily driven bad times. They do not have the notion of ethics, for them money bonus on the human person and the relationship between humans. It is as if in our country people like them. To understand just a little thing, you'll find people willing to say and do anything as long as their interests are safeguarded, while forgetting they are in front of a human being who deserves respect. The notion of love of neighbor does not seem to be well understood and controlled, it may be because it is not taught well by those who are supposed to do or simply application problem as it always was in our country, where we often have great ideas but in the application problem.

In addition to this first observation relates to the nature of our citizens, we must also consider the absence and the inability of our government to enforce the law as it should be at all. For us, this is the jungle that is to say where each is doing his law unmolested by anyone either, if it is a little frica is the worst.

About Commissionaries

ABIBU spoke to his father and said:

- Why the commissioner to which the State has assumed the responsibility to mediate between property owners or purchasers or tenants and furniture, they do not do their role properly?

- Why do they walk unnecessarily clients looking for property, furniture or any home, even if they do not have it, please?

- Why do they use cunning and crafty to deceive and defraud people desiring their services in collusion with the owners of these goods and furniture?

Speaking the father responds:

Our porters are those people who live to their services to property owners and those who want them. As two intermediate groups, they have an obligation to both sides wholes sets at home, so that there are no claims after the contract. Unfortunately, what we see on the ground, it is a different story.

Taking advantage of disorder, discord, anarchy prevailing in our country where everyone believes himself to be the master, the king, the president, the god in his field where he plot of responsibility; forwarders their tower can do anything in swindling money from third complicity with the holders of such goods and furniture. They think that by doing so, they earn more than if they were honest. That is why this practice is gaining more and more ground among agents.

About enterprises and companies

ABIBU turned to her and said:

- Why, businesses and companies that we consider structures of production of goods and services, employing people as employees or workers to accompany and support the economy, they assume this responsibility as it should be?

- Why, goods and services are more of a class of wealthy people, see abroad to the detriment of the population of the population which is the first beneficiary?

- Why, their workers are often victims of abuse or terminated without valid reasons and times for personal antipathy or because of any affiliation?

Speaking, the father responds:

Most companies that we belong here at home to expatriates or foreigners. By this we must understand that if a stranger or just install the expatriate business in our country, it certainly comes first for profit; unlike a son of his country, investing in their own country, although benefits but it is also the desire to help and promote his countrymen. Faced with a state that almost does not exist in its governance is weak, becomes an opportunity or a means by which these foreigners or expatriates mainly use to mistreat, abuse our people. They become untouchable suites their support from civil and military authorities of our country, who agree upon an amount to cover these business leaders even if they transgress the laws of the country. These supports make them assigns, privileged and so on. The people who work there is then abandoned to its own fate. The consequence is that the country is not moving and the people as another form of slavery.

About traditional chiefs.

ABIBU spoke to his father and said:

- Why the traditional chiefs to whom their ancient power was given officially and legally, that protect their human and material heritage, they do not take this task seriously heavy?

- Why, they get carried away or influenced by third parties animated bad times to destroy the inheritance, just to serve their own selfish interests?

- Why do not they wear their ancestral power to distract and confuse any plan to destroy the country, as was the case once?

Traditional leaders that we have today in our country no longer take their full role as protector of the city once. For several reasons whether political, economic and others. Accession to this position is not may not be according to the norms and rules that govern our traditional settings. Those who access traditional power do not follow the tradition of both the letter by lack of knowledge, either through negligence will manifest due to unethical practices to which they are subjected by those who helped him reach this position. Most chiefs have become politicians.

Thus, they act more like traditional authority called upon to establish peace and justice, but as a politician of our country, they seek power for power, that is to say, a power to serve its own interests detriment of the people and they cling to remain as long as possible even if the people do not want them anymore.

About spouses

ABIBU has a look at his father and said:

- Why, the spouse to whom the load and the power attributed to them by the Creator, custom and legislators directing their homes, they do not adequately fulfill this responsibility?

- Why do not they take seriously the burden for families that their homes become really basic cells for the development of our country?

- Why children do not recognize their primary responsibility as more, so they feel more fulfilled and secure their future?

Spouses in families are men with a religious marriage contract or civil or traditional. Through this contract, the man committed to God, family, the state to take in marriage the daughter of another family to live together, to form his own home. Once this is reached, the man takes authority over his wife and children they have in their friendship. But in our present, this practice is becoming a problem, because men do not have enough means to support and ensure the survival of his home. The few men who work do not have good wages can cover both ends of months and the vast majority of unemployed men live the worst. With such a situation, the spouses are difficult to fully do their role in the home. Those who find something to give to their homes, they waste a lot of time trying to live for it and they have little time to take care of their homes, because they are both the pluralist and those who 'find any lack of authority because they become dependent on their wives and even their children are doing in one way or another. Such as prostitution for girls. This situation means that the spouses become irresponsible face to their homes.

About wives

ABIBU turned to his father and said:

- Why wives who as a partner or assistant had been assigned next to their husbands for family welfare, seems to be ignored?

- Why, they have lost their place as mistress of the family who once cared about coaching and the future of their children, the fruit of their love?

- Why do they become resigned today from their homes and assume more properly their task master as it should be?

Wives are married women who have an obligation to respect their husbands whatever be their social ranks and ensure the smooth running of their homes alongside their partners husbands. Following the unfortunate situation that our country is in almost all areas, it is felt in the daily lives of our homes.

The two partners were not adequately prepare them to live together and do each role in the home, they get confused easily and especially with the economic crisis, they lose control any notion that they could have previously. Because women in general are weak creatures by nature, swayed, swept away by the wind political, economic and social. Just as the woman notices that her husband become financially weak, it will be an opportunity for the bride to disobey it and especially if it works or she manages to feed the family, it will seek to take the lead. That is to say, control and decide instead of her husband, who is just a label. A necessity, the woman or the wife considers either as a companion or assistant but as a decision maker instead of his male partner, her husband.

About children or young

ABIBU spoke to his father and said:

- Why do young people or children in whom rests the hope of tomorrow, do not take seriously the responsibility that awaits them?

- Why do not behave with dignity faced the company now has a negative outlook and remains pessimistic about their future?

- Why, they get caught up in practices that do not honor them such as: alcoholism, smoking, ease, theft, rape and others, and they will not listen to adults?

The father responds by saying:

You children or young people today, you are really different and unique compared to past generations. This generation differs from the old in evil. In our time, it was difficult to a child or young person to behave badly in front of everyone. There was a kind of gene faced to itself and its environment. Any one who badly behave, expect a severe punishment in the long run could only discourage him.

Having understood that the state has become resigned throughout the area, they each act according to his will, his aspiration without any reservation. As parents themselves are not able of taking responsibility for their children because of lack the financial resources due to unemployment and bad payment which they are victims, the children feel abandoned to their fate and support. This support makes them free beings. Not having the mastery of this freedom, they get caught up in the debauchery.

Laurent Lokwa Tshimbeka

About abandoned children

ABIBU turned to his father and said:

- Why, abandoned children that we consider as victims of injustice, the injustice of our leaders, parents and other societal structures that have made them what they are today, are- they unaware of their condition?

- Why do not they try to plead their case to the competent authorities, to ensure they arrive home just as their future?

- Why do they accept to be manipulated and fooled every time by malicious men, which exposes them and encourage them to evil for their own interests?

Reacted the father: Abandoned children you see here are in most cases from families, but due to a problem for one reason or another, they are abandoned in the street. Usually these reasons are known, either due to the poverty of parents, divorce, witchcraft declared false men of God. Once the child is rejected, he went to live on the street because it is difficult even to other members of his extended family to accept especially if said sorcerer.

Where his only place of refuge will the street where he himself became responsible for his fate. As in the street you live according to the principle of "every man for himself and God for all." The child's future is threatened by evil because there is no one who can help him. Therefore, it is obliged to do everything possible to find something to eat to live.

That is to say, how wholes are permitted provided that is enough to survive.

Taking this opportunity, ABIBU also seeks to know the explanation of some proverbs had in his head.

He turned to his father and said: what means this proverb: "Sit with a pretty girl and it seems you take a minute. It is the relativity"

The father explained:

Having to stand closed to a pretty girl pushes man to remain long contemplating the beautiful creature and it makes him forget many things, among others, the time seems to go faster.

ABIBU: "Put your hand on a stove for a minute and it will seem like an hour"

Father:

The pain felt by placing the hand on a stove for just a minute is not overlooked because it can cause you more trouble.

ABIBU:

"He who has planted a tree before dying needlessly has not lived"

Father:

The Planting a tree is one way to show its age, its history and its existence because this tree used to his contemporaries and to future generations. Hence it is important for every human being to leave the trail to mark his time and memory use for future generations.

ABIBU:

"The truth is on the top of the beyond"

Father:

The truth trumps all realities. This is with the truth that man can truly be free. So the truth is the virtue that frees man and makes him truly man. A man who does not live in the truth is not a free man because he is someone who always has a guilty conscience. That is to say that it is the criticism always something in his own conscience, despite all appearances he can manifest.

ABIBU:

"No retirement is more or less disturbed to peaceful man that he finds in his soul"

Father:

The soul of man is the place per excellence which is peace, tranquility, for a human being. The man may have everything but if his soul is not in peace, the man can not be happy. In short, the happiness of man is conditioned by his soul.

ABIBU:

"People need happiness and unhappiness to walk in balance"

Father:

A balanced man is not only those who live in the enjoyment but also one who knows how to face the difficulties and sufferings. Because it is through these difficulties that man discovers and directs his life. Happiness and unhappiness are essential in the life of a man because there are no roses without thorns.

ABIBU:

"Man needs day and night to live in balance"

Father:

Day and night are two moments indispensable for human life. These two moments can also mean enjoyment and suffering. Day as the moment of enjoyment and night as the time of suffering. These two points can mean more roses and thorns with the roses as the day and night like thorns. So the man's interest to consider two times to balance.

ABIBU:

"If you persist by turning back on the reality, happiness and unhappiness slide out your heart like torrent water of pebbles"

Father:

A Man shall not live by ignoring the realities of life around him. If he chooses to go to the nature or reality, it will eventually lose.

ABIBU:

"A wise man can be neither govern nor seeks to govern the others because he wants the reason govern alone and always"

Father:

A wise man is the one who let reason prevail over all. That is to say the reason must take the front of his feelings and actions. Because the brain uses engine and sits on top of everything.

ABIBU:

"The highest degree of human wisdom is knowing bend his character and the circumstances make an interior calm despite the storms outside"

Father:

Human wisdom advises us to be humble and to develop a strong personality to face the trials because before honor is humility. And face hardships, it takes some self-control. By doing so we can say to achieve the highest degree of human wisdom.

ABIBU:

"Happiness indeed is the wisdom and dreaming is happiness"

Father:

Happiness can be acquired only by a wise man and the dreaming happiness, it is the beginning of wisdom because a wise man is a happy man. This is a man who knows how to transform these dreams into action for his happiness and that of his entourage because a wise man does not live for himself but also for others.

ABIBU:

"I know mens who pass for wises only because they do not say anything"

Father:

A wise man is not the one who talks a lot but often it is those who know how to be silent because silence is a great asset to a wise man. A wise man is the one who speaks little and listens much and he knows when to speak.

ABIBU:

"We must flee without turning the company of the wicked"

Father:

Once when we decided to flee the bad company, we have to go without turning back because that is likely to experience the worst.

ABIBU:

"The wise man follow the absence of pain and not pleasure"

Father:

A wise man is not the one who seeks pleasure because pleasure is linked to the body, been a wise man is to follow the total satisfaction, not partial. That is to say, the tranquility of his mind and his body.

ABIBU:

"Appearances are beautiful in their momentary truth"

Father:

Appearances always reflect the truth momentary and superficial because the real truth is revealed over time. So we can not rely on appearances if we really want to achieve the reality or the real truth.

ABIBU:

"Those whose their only desire is to achieve never know where they're going"

Father:

When one embarks on an adventure when you do not know what it may lead us. That is to say, we can know the time of the beginning of something but its purpose is we both strange and elusive.

ABIBU:

"Who lives without folly is not so wise as he thinks"

Father:

It takes time in life to avoid being too charismatic, he must be a happy medium. That is to say, avoid believing always know everything, you may be more ignorant.

ABIBU:

"He who is not progressing every day retreats every day"

Father:

Life has no meaning if there is no evolution. The man who remains static is doomed to extinction, because there is no development without growth.

ABIBU:

"Wanting to be someone else, and like everyone else he will never be a person"

Father:

Someone who underestimates is not a man because a man is the one who accepts and assumes that to create its own personality.

ABIBU:

"To be desperate, he must have lived good and still love the world"

Father:

A desperate man is he who, after having lived a long time and have not been satisfied, becomes despair because it is difficult for a child to have that feeling of despair.

ABIBU:

"Happiness indeed, is all wisdom. And dreaming is happiness"

Father:

A happy man is above all a wise man. A wise man is a provision and a provision is a man who has a vision from afar.

ABIBU:

"What is now proved was once only imagined by"

Father:

What the world is today has been created by our predecessors. So there is no hazard in what we are and what we live and see.

ABIBU:

"There must attach to a resolution because it is good, not because it has been chosen"

Father:

We can not attach to a resolution if it is not good because it was chosen. We attach to a decision whether it is good and if it is not good, it would be best to withdraw.

ABIBU:

"Only the tree that has withstood the onslaught of the wind is really strong because it is in this struggle that has its roots tested to strengthen"

Father:

This is in front of events that man discovers and becomes mature. A man without experience is not yet mature and responsible. One becomes after facing many trials.

ABIBU:

"The advantage of the pain is that it gives you the will to change and this is the same profit"

Father:

The pain is not only suffering but also a way to help us to change. That is to say we must not only see the pain in his negative side because it also has its positive side, it whose brings man to change his kind of being.

TITLE V

THE WORKER

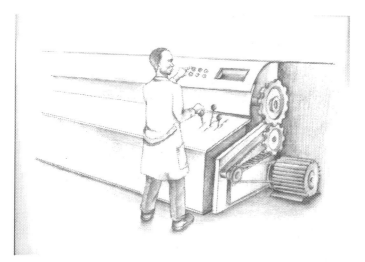

ABIBU after removal of the convent, he was difficult to adapt to city life. His parents were no longer able to send him studying at university. His maternal uncle and maternal aunt who use to help his mother for his studies, had lost all their job. To try to ease the burden to his parents, he decided to move the contest to recruit new teachers in a complex-school in his neighborhood. At the end of the event, will be retained as a teacher of the orientation of the school. That is to say it should be taught in first and second secondary classes including some of the third humanity. The young teacher will support full-time schedule with civics, drawing, physical education and English due to his training done in a language learning center.

This commitment to quality teaching was for him not only a way to support themselves, but also as an early professional experience. To this end the young man should take it seriously. Thus he will begin training seminar scheduled by the sponsor and the school principal. Curiously, the first day of the seminar ABIBU noticed that he was the youngest of all the teachers and they were surprised to see among them. At the end of the seminar, the young Recrut gained the confidence of everyone in his way of being, his knowledge, his wisdom and intelligence.

At the start of classes, ABIBU will again be curiosity, astonishment of students presenting their youngest teacher. Some doubted his credibility, his ability to teach others and even mocked him. The young teacher meanwhile, was more focused, concerned with the responsibilities that have been entrusted by his superiors and that he had trusted. After all these ceremonies the school year, all promotions and all the classrooms that had received were amazed by his intelligence, his eloquence, his knowledge and so many other qualities had their young teacher that well 'there were still some students who still hesitated to believe to him.

Over time, ABIBU began to adapt his job, as well as students trusted him completely. He became the most popular and most beloved of all faculty.

With this popularity, it was hard to him to miss school, even if he had not of course, he had to come because he was demanded by all. When he came, it was not with the idea to claim any salary or payment of overtime, but if he did it was by his passion and profession with the idea of pleasing hundreds of people who loved him.

This situation does not enchanted other spirits with whom he worked together, not having a valid reason to start young because he was perfect, but almost every model. After several attempts and tests they found a weak point, the fact that it lacked an academic title. They took advantage of this weakness to make noise to higher authorities, according to which anyone who has no academic title shall in no case avail himself especially not teach secondary and humanities despite its qualities.

This information will be sent to the ears of inspectors, who also did not want to be punished by the high command, decided to leave the young teacher that liked them all. As the verdict fell, the governing body had trouble announce the decision in their young employee, but eventually he know. To calm the situation, they found a formula that the authorities wanted to see the poor young teacher will return with an academic title.

So that the situation does not worsen with students, given its popularity, they asked the person to accurately convey this decision to his students. Taking courage, ABIBU acted as had been recommended. Despite these procedures, it had created a certain tension on the part of students, who did not agreed to this decision. This situation provoked and caused several departures of students to other institutions. As the young man was a fatal blow to his life, who after two months he had touched his salary he felt already autonomous and responsible faced most of his family, because with his meager salary he supported his family as little self. So back to unemployment, it was an ordeal for him. And as he should not remain in this state of unemployment, he decided one day to take a ride on the side of the center where he learned English. Upon his arrival, he met the head of the center who was his French teacher of the humanities. Taking advantage of this meeting ABIBU told of his situation and what had happened to him. And his former teacher, who was also looking for someone trustworthy to replace his former secretary who left following the hijacking. It was a happy coincidence for the teacher and center manager because he knew his former student whom he loved and appreciated once. Profited to the occasion, he proposed that vacancy. For the young man was an extraordinary grace and he did not hesitate to give his assent.

At the moment the teacher-student discourse became an employee speech. This discourse mission was to provide guidance to the work. At the end of this meeting, an employment contract was signed. Although he started his job the next day, but he found important to keep secret even from his family. His desire in this decision because he wanted to touch everything before his first paycheck.

His family had suspected his movements and as they had no evidence because there was nothing they said, despite their insistence, remained all observers. Although in the beginning always been difficult ABIBU be adapted easily to his new job, which was to collect fees for participation in training and trained with help prevent absent or trainers to hold valid candidates.

Thus, he worked from morning to night because as he had also given all the keys, it should come before everyone else and leave the latter as long as it closes all the doors. He could sit and put something in their mouths as the space of time that separated vacation ahead than the afternoon to finish in the evening. Sunday was his only day of rest.

To preserve his health, he was forced to sacrifice other activities and commitments he had at the church where he prayed. Again the young assistant secretary and became more and more popular by her professionalism, expertise and intelligence especially in the transmission of lessons. Confident of its performance, the current head homeroom entrusting one of its courses, including the hourly load was lower. Although this small holder literacy classes, he continued to perform his former duties cover other trainers.

As this was not enough his former teacher gave him the swallows begin to deposit the money collected in the general direction. He was young and unmarried among all his colleagues, he was subjected to provocation of all young girls who were desperate to be in love with them. For these candidates, ABIBU was exceptional trainer, ideal reference with whom they could share their experiences in love, because he had the qualities required of a good husband. Wholes means were then brought into play as long as they attract the attention of their target. Unlike the customs of his society where the relationship is often the man who takes the initiative in the first place, but in his case, the girls ran behind him instead.

Despite several attempts, the young trainer remained constant and categorical behavior. He rubbed everyone unpretentious fall in love with a girl. This reserve could be explained by the fact that according to him it was not the time to embark on this adventure. Faced to his service colleagues who some malicious, to sink, he asked for the loan exaggerated even encouraged to diversion. For them, the wages they received did not match the given work.

So the only way out of this situation was especially rigged received. A situation that does not enchanted the center's director, his former teacher. Thus there were two cases opposed to the center. Each group tended to attract ABIBU on his side, but he was neither for nor against any group, because he was a craftsman of the unit rather than division. This conflict was for him an opportunity to make his ministry as a Christian. Although it was not an easy task, but it was not pessimistic because according to his understanding it was not impossible.

To achieve this he chose in the first place impartiality as a way to challenge and secondly sharing the word of God that he brought from his home to his daily meditations. It was so at every opportunity that presented itself, he did not hesitate to urge them all. Given his insistence and perseverance, both groups expect finally by talking and spoke the same language. This expectation had advanced their center in the whole area and they attracted many more applicants. Instead to be proud like the young peacemaker merely to congratulate and encourage the two groups exceeded they have feelings and passions. They continued in this atmosphere until the day when the young man decided to leave for another opportunity that had been proposed.

ABIBU be hired as a marketer agent in the company of a fellow businessman, who was the sub-contractor of a large manufacturing company and selling tobacco. The man was responsible for the distribution and sale of cigarettes. Given the heavy responsibility he had, he should engage personnel may accompany the completion of his task. It is because of this that the young man had been hired. A commitment that had not been easy because it took several tricks to make it successful.

The work assigned to him as an agent of the marketer was taking cartons of cigarettes from his first motorcycle and send to resellers. Therefore, he had this thing to him as his other colleagues of service. That is to say, the bike remained with him and he used it even for his private courses, provided it does not touch the fuel reserved for racing society. For four consecutive years, ABIBU was accustomed to the pace of work was not at all easy, but he had to adapt to survive with his family. One day after a misunderstanding or bad waited with his superiors, the decision fell from above for his dismissal and other colleagues of service.

Despite their justification, the decision was upheld and enforced as such. Left to themselves, limited by the means they did not know what to do because the law of retaliation record in full swing, that the fittest was always the best. That is to say until we have money, we can even walk on the law of the country. In other words, men Friques, influential were above the law. While the unfortunate colleagues undertook legal proceedings to establish the company in their right; ABIBU had not committed simply because he knew it would not lead to a good result. Despite the stress of the pots, the young man remained adamant and said he did not want to lose the little that remained to justice. A justice who was serving wealthy and against the people of lower class.

It was during this period that anxiety is crafted a new opportunity to the young. Was called by the way of one of his friend the to do the same job he was doing before. He went to work to sign a contract and he forgot definitely the file of his former boss.

This new opportunity was a new life, a new beginning and a new impetus for ABIBU, because he would be able to help his family and prepare for the future. For he had resumed his work marketer, although in another company he tore most markets belonged to his former boss. His exploits were the result of his exemplary behavior, honest and humble faced to their clients. Having learned this feat of his former employee, former boss looked for ways to reinstate dismissed employee using his emissaries to defeat, but it was a failure. And when the new boss heard the news, he called his new employee personally.

In welcoming the foremost consistent with an envelope, he exhorted him to do better and promised him good things. ABIBU turn first thanked his current boss gesture he asks for it and then he noted that feasibility if he wants to stay in his company, it is the consideration and confidence believed to benefit him and his aides.

On this occasion, he promoted his new boss, a job well done in all conscience if things remain as he finds now. In short, each party respecting its commitments faced the other. It is in this climate of mutual trust that the parties had undertaken to accomplish each task. A few years later, everyone had the constant positive returns at the base ABIBU. This does not leave indifferent the head. He promised bonus and promotion to young new marketer and his team.

This promise was not enchanted circle of the head because they feared a likely replacement position. Whenever the team of marketers wanted to start any process for their bonuses and promotions, they saw themselves thwarted by the entourage of the head. The team surrounding chief had already organized for these promises are not met. While the team of marketers do not realize the plot because they thought it was an administrative problem. Why the group multiply their efforts in order to be established in their prerogative.

As hanging out, because of their right to seek and credits, all opted for this alternative. Their opponents found through this option, a safer way to drive in the marketers agents even from work. For this, they were organized to provide credit exorbitant, extravagant and for an indefinite period with targeted agents. This approach was only to try to trap the group ABIBU who considers the head by the way they work.

Content of this offer bomb, they each took turns and according to his needs. About ABIBU, although it was not warm and interested in this offer, but limited by his conflict with his landlord rental, he was forced to contract. With this amount, he went to find another house to rent in the nearby town. Wise he was, he was the one to take the lower amount compared to others.

Three months later, when all seemed well between labor market. Agents marketers were surprised by a recall order from their commanders administrators asked them to pay their debts in a short time for fear that it costs them dearly. This approach challenges the ABIBU group because he not return from the reaction of the hierarchy of their department.

Wanting to try to understand the essence, the foundation of this warning, they understood that it was a problem of antipathy, jealousy on the part of their leaders after a thorough investigation. Also wanting to position, but it was already too late because the ground was already undermined by strategies of their potential adversaries. One day, while ABIBU was going around with his bike through his work, he sent a message that it was heard in the office before he goes to his home. Arrival at the meeting, he found his colleagues, who were also called to the same cause. Curiously, they found that it was their group that was arrested. It is beyond they took seriously their calling. The number is reached, they invited everyone in the office to inform them they were under arrest for failing to honor their commitment, at the same time saw five policemen enter and rushed towards them.

On orders from their superiors, they embarked on a jeep that was outside as criminals and thieves. They stripped him of everything they had as private property and left their bikes abandoned. Wanting to know why this kind of treatment, the police brutally and savagely retaliated by saying that it was not their business because they were just trying to execute the order from the hierarchy. So they had to be quiet and wait for their verdict. They accompanied them in a military camp in the square to the late hours. Arrival in the camp, they brought them right into a prison where they keep the recalcitrant military and police. They had been treated the same way.

The next morning, they forwarded them directly to the floor. Meanwhile their families began to search for them. They learned after several stunts that their were in one of the public prosecutor of the city. Turn it was to travel all the public prosecutor and they found them. Seeking to meet them, they demanded to pay bail. Once paid, they just gave them a few minutes not exceeding 10 minutes.

According to the habits of the around and regulations in place, the vehicle's central prison used to the beginning and towards the end of the week to recover defendants convicted confirmed by the judgments of magistrates. To prevent their not found in the case of imprisonment, each family organized its way to release its acknowledgment. All failed to do the same day. The next day, they met for repeat procedures for the release of their family members arrested. They went defense lawyers from the friend of the sister of ABIBU. This association colleagues to the cause of their clears. With this combination, the families of the accused had not spent as they believed. God willing, after trial ABIBU and his colleagues won the trial and were released late in the afternoon.

This victory was very unpopular in the other camp, because their leaders who had accused, the case should lead into the central prison. As it was not the case, it was a question of looking for other strategies. Then they were waiting at the time of their claim-final liquidation account. At the end of the hearing the prosecutor, the victorious saw a few seek civil and military dignitaries. The main reason was to grab their case in order to get money to this company because they understood that these workers had great reason. They came to an agreement for cooperation and made an appointment in a week time they gather the evidence needed to confront their managers.

Before the day of the appointment arrived, wise he was, and inquired ABIBU consultation with others better placed in this field about their problem. Among these persons consulted, there was a labor inspector who advised him not to go to meet these high civil and military. He says going to them, it will be a waste of time and money because they will eventually land home. Thus had offered him to bring the matter directly to them.

The young man went to inform his colleagues of reality and they came to an agreement to go directly to the labor inspectorate. To get rid of these group of dignitaries, despite their good intentions to help, they sought a pretext financial argument and the case was concluded from that side.

The opponent meanwhile, was also on their way. Strategy as they stopped spinning their enemies. A strategy that had answered favorably because they understood that their enemies had referred the case to the General Labour Inspectorate. To work around and end this issue, particularly fear that their boss is informed and challenged. They negotiate with a police commander in charge of its elements attached to another public prosecutor of the city. With them they walked together first vehicle with the goal of removing their enemies. Something said and done, they surprised them one day while they were leaving the General Labour Inspectorate. They rushed towards them and they embarked on their first brutally vehicle of its complicity corrupt police. As they were well armed person could not intervene to oppose them and they brought them to an unknown destination.

Surprised by such a criminal act done in front of and eyeness to everyone during a day. These inspectors decided to lend a hand to his innocent. All mobilized to advocate and bring justice to these poor people. Knowing the seriousness of the case and also being well organized, especially since they were financially strong, they almost wholes corrupted judges that prosecutors who held their file, so that their enemies do not linger. That is to say, once arrived they are sent directly to Central Prison.

But unfortunately after the noise made by the inspectors denouncing the kidnapping wild with a group of workers in a certain company of which he is the victim and the case turned sour against the sponsors of this kidnapping. Men right of low got also the case. The implementation of the problem posed folder as expected.

After several investigations victims were found. They stopped all sponsors and order of their boss, they were tried and convicted several years in Central Prison. ABIBU and his colleagues were rehabilitated in their rights and they returned to their jobs.

TITLE VI

THE LOVER

ABIBU returned from the convent after withdrawing himself from where he had spent several years training. This experience had discovered several cultures and realities of life through trips from one province to another, from one country to another. He traveled these areas with different means of transport, sometimes in a canoe, boat, bike, motorcycle, vehicle or on board an aircraft.

To return to the family, saw all that he had acquired as training and experience, the youth was difficult to find. He could not believe it. He was dazzled, confused and disoriented. In short, he does not adapt to this lifestyle of his family and his environment. He was accustomed to a life of concentration, meditation and prayer, of order, of organization, of silence in short he was accustomed to a life where everything was regulated programmed. That is to say, chance and improvisation had no place. The new life he was forced to live already beginning to have repercussions and fallen on his mind, his psyche and his physical. He was in court for reflection. He could no longer think as it should be. So he was affected.

To break the deadlock after him, he was about to leave the community and go to live alone in the first place. But this idea was unrealistic at this time because the realization of this idea was influenced by financial means. But there was still nothing during this period. As the impossible nothing is held, he was content only with difficulty of this reality to heart and he kept his project. The day he found a job, after subjected to several tests, he decided the space of a week to move the middle. On leaving, he preferred to spend a few days before while in her maternal aunt, the youngest of his mother, bride and mother of a child more or less 10 years.

While the decision has not pleased everyone, but he was forced to leave. His stay at his aunt's goal was to enable it to meet a guarantee just a piece of home to rent in a common center, and also allow him to buy some goods for his new home, as some three plastic chairs, a table, a sponge and a single bed other. In the space of three months, he managed to meet the minimum he needed in the first place. After he met his property and found the piece in question, he announced his departure to his maternal aunt.

This announcement does not arranged his aunt, because according to her it was not for him to leave. In other words, the decision was too sudden and premature. ABIBU but eventually convince her maternal aunt decision, contrary to its design. The young man finally went to occupy his house as planned. After some time, he had the need for some one with whom he is occasionally exchange and may occasionally assist in daily tasks. Where he put his choice on a girl from the neighborhood where he lived by chance, because the meeting took place far from their neighborhood.

This proximity was a chance for him because they could see almost every day without much acrobatics. The girl had just barely get his bachelor's degree in a province in which the youth had esteem for his future wife. The said province was closest to the capital and it has a good reputation hence its morality. Thus ABIBU could not pass this opportunity and especially the lady appeared to fulfill the criteria that needed by its appearance. The affair began and they coasted.

According to the realities of the environment, the young man could not get the girl. Rather, it is she who should create the time slipped away and come home to his fraudulent partner who had his house with him. So their meeting place was the home of the young man. At first, they came to an agreement to said truths especially compared to their old relationships. Not having a past love issues, the fact that he had just returned from the convent, especially away from the capital, he contented himself over him about his religious education in the province where he came from.

As for his concubine, she recounted her past love with a man she had known when she began the humanities. At the time the guy was a student in a higher institute near their school. Just when he had finished his studies, he had moved in search of a job in another town than theirs. Since his departure, according to her, she had no friend or partner. So she lived alone without partner until the day when the two new lovers were encountered. It is through these truths both began their love affair and they turned the page with the old love stories.

A few months later, the girl began to make trips to the ancient city under the pretext of stresses sisters who need her to manage their daily business between the capital and their hometown. But in reality, it was not the reason. These trips were caused by herself to meet his former partner. She and the boys had organized that every time the boy returned from his trip, the girl should also return to that city.

Realizing she had two concubines in two different cities, it was so well organized to manage the relationship with her three older sisters, two of whom lived in their hometown and the capital with their parents. Whenever their young sister should be moving from one city to another. It was her sisters who informed the two concubines of their young sister. This approach aimed to cover their young sister in evil and protect the two guys. This system characterized their family and they were in it, because it allowed them to maintain their romantic relationships with several men as long as possible. It became a real network and they supported each other.

One day on the occasion of the feast of love, while her lover ABIBU and found themselves in their usual place to celebrate in their own way, as saying goes: "every thing to its end", it was also the end of double game played by the girl. While the lady took care of housework, a telephone message appeared to the phone of the girl. Unfortunately for the girl, and fortunately for the poor boy who had the device. Surprised by the contents of the text message staying that: "... although baby away from me, I know that this festival don't disturb you or worry in my absence where you are, because we're going to recover from my back in a few days and when you come to...as usual, doors and you well soon. I love you. Your love..."

This message appeared under the name of a correspondent located in the directory of the girl. That said matching was presented by the lady as his cousin the young man had never seen but often called the evening when they parted. Under this emotion and shock ABIBU calmly called his concubine coming to read his message. Reading the contents of the text message, the girl pretending feasibility and exclaimed with a smile guilt: "ah, this is a disturber."

Wanting to go about their occupation, but ABIBU adopted a serious look saying: "Whatever you mean has always been like your cousin, it allows the feast of love, to make you such a text message and you qualify of disturber! Yes she meets with an air guilty. At the moment, the young man became angry and changed the tone directly, saying, Who is there who can afford, it is not my partner like me, you do such a text!

Having realized that the affair took another look, she replied, trembling, "it was not a question of you angry, let me explain. The party in question is a cousin of extended family that I know of. He does not live here too, but in our hometown. I'm surprised that he send this message to me, I've always considered him like a member of my family. But through this SMS, I now realize its intentions and now I want to take away from him. So there is nothing between me and him."

The young man replied, "if so, I would call him for reprimanding to cease to bother you. This would be an opportunity or a way for you to once and for all rid of him." No question, his concubine energetically replied: "It is not up to you to solve this matter is to myself and my family to take care of." What is that! The boy responds: "where is the harm if I got involved in your case! Especially since some time some members of your family know me as your boy friend, it is my duty to put an end to this adventure." No question, replied once again his concubine: "You have no right to interfere with you my private affairs especially family." I want to do my assuming responsibility, replied the boy. Negative, she said.

Baby Birth immediately terrible misunderstanding between these two lovers because none of them wanted to concede their position. Just when ABIBU was about to call the guy with the phone from his concubine, it jumped on him to snatch the camera and they quarreled phone. During this time the phone rang and the correspondent picked up and answered.

The young man is stronger than the girl, he began to talk with his rival, who posed the question ABIBU "Who are you to talk on the phone with my baby? It is rather that I was going to ask you the question, what right you are allowed to send this text message to my concubine?".

As the girl was at all costs to stop this discussion and tear but it was difficult for her. Meanwhile, there was a terrible cacophony. That of the other author of this town waiting for the text message in his phone argument, recognizing the voice of his lover who was not with him. Rivals began to curse and the phone at the same time ABIBU arguing with his concubine.

Having realized that he really dealing with a rival, not a cousin as his lover had lied serious months, he began to hit him. It also does not leave and allowed to tear the clothes on top of the young man. This attracted the curiosity of neighbors, but still hesitated to intervene. Suddenly they saw coming a boy and friends rushed to him, while suggesting to quickly intervene.

Informed immediately, he went to them and separeted. His presence among them and calmed them, respect visitors all calmed down. Speaking, the visitor mediator, conciliator asked them the question: "What happened to you get to this level? ". Each in turn he recounted the event in its own way, but almost the same way. The Peacemaker tried to appease all with some advice. Both listened.

A few minutes later, the visitor improvised mediator, peacemaker asked his friend to accompany them to let girl, because it was already too late. Together they accompanied the problematic lady to where they used to separate. Return home ABIBU decided to discontinue this relationship with this girl. And his friend advised him to do so in a calm, in silence without the use of brutality. This would be a way to keep his honor, credibility and personality faced his entourage. Since that day the boy wisely withdrew his concubine problem. The side of the girl, she thought otherwise. That is to say, with the reconciliation effected on the date of the dispute was sufficient to renew their friendship. But there was no question to her partner, although he did not say clearly and directly.

A week later, used to traveling, she also announced as usual that she believed to be her partner again, her departure for that city at the request of her sisters.

Just leaving the daughter, the young man loved another girl. This act was a revenge for ABIBU to his former concubine. The one where there was, she noticed that his capital boy friend never called as before. But every time she tried to reach the phone, the other replied shyly with indifference in his statements. This attitude began to worry about where she was, but she thought maybe her partner in the capital had problems either at work or in the family or elsewhere, forgetting what she had done before her arrival in the city native.

One day when her partner tried to call in the evening after all day with that of the city where she was at that time, the way she hears a girl who answered: what can I do for you madame or miss, this is my girlfriend ABIBU. Wanted to stress the same person had remained online. Troubled, upset by this response, the former concubine doesn't sleep not all night because she did not return. When she tried to call her lover again, it confirmed the presence of her daughter as his new concubine.

Shocked by this announcement, the girl decided to interrupt his stay. Having the habit of seducing boys, she applied all her seduction strategies to regain her place. Besides, one day before returning it remained in constant contact with her boy friend. She announced her decision to spend the next day path through the way of his friend peacemaker.

Curiously, despite the advice of his friends asked him to no longer live with the girl, the young man decided to recover her. The two came to an agreement to implement their decision on the day of the arrival of the girl. That day came and the two new lovers met themselves at the bus park as agreed. From there, they went straight to their usual place of meeting with all baggage of rehabited girl

That day, it was a great meeting of the two lovers. Forgetting the past, they celebrated the event in style. At night the boy went larger house than the current one. The next day late in the afternoon, the girl went to her partner. While they were sitting talking, they heard someone knocked on their door insistently. Going to see, ABIBU found himself facing his second girlfriend, barely lived together, which also came to visit. Not wanting to create a scandal, faced with this situation, the young prohibits his second visitor who was accompanied by his girlfriend not to enter in the house. Surprised by this decision, she replied that since we met, this is my very first time you hold me in about the same. This is due to what and what does it mean?

There is not looking for the whys and wherefores of this decision, replied the boy, the only reason is that I am now busy with another person. Pursuing it, your presence would be an inconvenience because we have serious things to talk about. As the visitor outside the house wanted to enter, it attracted the curiosity of those inside who approached the door to realize. At the minute, tension mounted between the two rivals. This by the fact that the inside of the house wanted to know who was at the door with her partner who spoke person and why she insisted so much! And the visitor was also curious person was inside the home with her partner. This situation created a mess and a serious misunderstanding and attracted the curiosity of neighbors.

To calm the situation, the young man was imposed in the middle of them and ordered one that was inside the house and go to the outside to stay there, it s time 'ready to accompany them. Both executed. Along the way while the other was left alone in the house, ABIBU said to that was accompanied by her girlfriend, he was not available these days to meet, as he had business to settle with his alleged rival. This is to say that it was unnecessary for her to come get him, but when he finishes with the other he will sign. At these words they parted, although the lady and her companion was struggling to understand their speaker. In return, he found one that was at his home with a knife and very angry. The young man calmed down and explained to the girl why he had come to do so. At the end, they forgave and it was a new start for a new friendship.

Meanwhile the embargo which had multiplied opportunities to meet, but it will eventually fail, despite the interventions of his relatives. A few months later, the girl recovered is brought with a new topic. Assertion that it should travel with their father to attend a customary marriage of her older sister. Informed of the new, the young man became discouraged while trying to revive the film past. Not having the power to prohibit as his concubine to travel, especially as it was the father to the girl who organized, nothing could be thought or prevent this trip. It was a great sorrow from the boy who accepted him despite this trip.

In the words of the girl, it was a trip of a week was what calmed ABIBU. But a week after the father of his concubine returned alone. Calling the question, she says she heard go with her nieces and nephews who should get their holiday that side. Continuing justification tell her sisters she did not want to leave for fear that their children do not fall alone. While the boy continued to wait in the capital, serious things were getting ready on the other side of the province. The boy heard from the old friend of his concubine, had announced a date for the ceremony her family pre-dote. In his impatience, the young man ventured one day call his concubine to discuss about her return, he heard from the mouth of the person concerned she would not return these days because she was doing its efforts to its inclusion in the Higher Institute of way. Wanting to know why this decision when there were already upstream approaches and outstanding swallows it began more! Sorry, replied the girl, that my decision comes not from me, but my family. Given the cost that it would engage in the capital, they took their choice for my hometown and I could not oppose this decision. So we can keep our friendship even remotely. Never, replied the boy and he unhooked phone. Since that day it was the end of this friendship and decided not to live in friendship with a girl who often travels from one medium to another.

TITLE VII

THE TENANT

ABIBU already bored to continue living with his mother and two younger brothers in a room with two bedrooms and a living room, lying side by side with other rooms occupied by tenants of his maternal aunt, owner of the parcel. The realities of life accompanied by repeated bad language, do not enchanted young man, who had just returned from the convent after five (5) years of training in religious life. Without means, he could not but he took to heart his decision to leave the place.

A day at evening, after the meeting at the parish for the frame of youth MONIMAMBO, his intimate friend brought him information that there is a company who recruit new workers tomorrow through an entrance examination. At the same time, they prepared to face this test tomorrow morning.

As they lived in the outskirts of the city province, they decided to spend night together and to 05 o'clock they took the bus to the city center, where the test should take place. A few meters, they found a huge crowd of over a thousand men and a few women in the workforce. All start to look forward to the arrival of the team in charge of this event. Instead of being discouraged, they mutually motivated to face that test while following instructions received loan while the message they had been sent.

To 8 o'clock 'they two vehicles came into the intended location. A white man and a few national down to collect gear the crowd around them. They asked to match the order of size that is to say, the more passes and most giant remains behind. It is this order that our friends disperse because they did not have the same size.

The test had four steps:

The first was to eliminate those who did not obey the instructions given: wearing shoes with socks, shaved beards, holding down town with ties and others.

The second was related to the interview in English for those who speak English and French for those who do not know English, who had a special character.

The third focused on the written test psychosomatic.

The fourth was devoted to training.

The last reserved last test recall of the training acquired

ABIBU franchisees all these steps, but MONIMAMBO stopped somewhere and wished good luck to his friend, who will be among the winners. A few days later, the staff director of the company summoned them to start work. Given the distance and time of work, which had been imposed, the young man decided shortly after to go and live with his mom younger, married and mother of a resident to another little town close with ease transport from its place of work.

Going to live with his maternal aunt, his goal was to bring a rental guarantee and buy some staffs for his future home. After six months, he managed to meet those they needed and thus crafted approaches to the question for rent. ABIBU contact from one of those friends living in the municipality of the city center, which in turn led to a commission in the matter. With him, they went through all avenues of the district in which the young man wanted to live. As agreed, once access is given to the commission, it will be expired until his client will find the desired part.

A few days later, he found a piece of the value of his security deposit. This house was a studio, that is to say one piece. To enter, you should wait nearly two more months, the time for the person who had the house moved. The person was his landlord, who is a child of the deceased owner of the parcel. The house should occupy ABIBU is a compartment big house with other compartments inherited by each child. Not yet ready at the agreed date, his future landlord asked a few more days to the tenant, which is already impatient. Finally home had been released at the request of ABIBU, the wife of his friend will prepare the house cleaner systematically.

On the eve of his departure ABIBU talked to her maternal aunt and her husband, he said: Papa and Mama leki except last minute change, barring unforeseen tomorrow, I think I can leave you for starting my life like a man, because I found a house to rent. At this stage I can only thank you for everything you have done for me. Continuing this conversation in a family atmosphere accompanied by advice from his officials circumstance.

The next day after work, he brought his staffs in his new residence and other items had been overtaken by the woman the wife of his friend. With three plastic chairs, he set up his parlor and sponge in her room a separate curtain. His stove plate, six plates and two pots from his mother including her some utensils were most of his kitchen. In the plot were the widow, her children, grandson and two other tenants whose married with one child and the other with five (5) children.

His presence attracted the attention of other residents who came to greet him turn while advising him especially compared to the attitude to adopt face other residents of the plot. He was unmarried, to cook, he called his girlfriend, who lived in a municipality other than his own. Prepared meals should serve him for three days, but each should himself prepared the leg or fufu or rice, potatoes to accompany the food prepared. Other housework were provided by himself.

Concerned about the situation ABIBU, the widow called him and said, Dad, I always see how you bothering with housework in your house without your friend. This situation has never left indifferent, that's why I propose to call my little girls to help you with this, because I consider, she said, as your little sisters and they never refuse to accommodate you. Joyfully ABIBU accepted and thanked grandmother for this gesture of generosity towards her. But before his execution, he participated in the feasibility girlfriend, who in turn gave her swallow with some conditions. Since that day, a family atmosphere reigned between ABIBU and the family of her donor in mutual respect. This pushed the boy to consider this family as his second family, although it was not his country than he. The atmosphere and also continued until the day he should leave the house for a bigger one than this. Then he went away again contact his former broker, the pastor.

Have been requested and promised another job with a reasonable salary. The studio ABIBU begins to clutter. As his commissioner take time to find him a home and living room. ABIBU went to meet other commissioners, but unfortunately he fell into the hands of bad employees, thirsty for money. They gave him a house at night in a swamp area and exposed to flooding. He was pressed and lack of experience in the field and in the manner of flattery raven, the young man agreed to occupy and filler all the formalities on the same night.

Two weeks after his predecessor was released home, ABIBU settled. He held the door in the middle, having as his colleague next right and left neighboring tenant to the landlord polygamous two women with a dozen children. One day to night during the month of November, a period of the rainy season. A heavy rain was falling while ABIBU sleeping peacefully with his young brother, his friend and his young brother to his friend. Suddenly they heard noises from outside: wake up, wake up, water is going to break into your home.

At the moment young peoples woke up and began to prevent the penetration of water into the house, but not having experience in the field, the water overflowed and flooded the whole house looks helplessly to our young people. That's when they decided to make up all the stuff and allergic perishable and water as the water level recovered hip, they spent the second half of the night on the window while the rain continued the right path; they satdown on the wall and the window with their feet in the flood water, waiting for the end of the rain and the reduction or diminution of water, which intervened until the morning.

About their neighbor lessor experienced and familiar with the situation, had already made arrangements with his family to protect their property as they have always used.

Morning none of the four youngs could get that service to the university and to the store. They all stayed at home to try to clean the house and all property flooded and damaged by the flood. Hard work that occupied almost the whole day just to find living space and many days to get the house in order, because there were stuff that should be dried in the sun for days.

Faced with this unpleasant surprise, ABIBU contemplated the possibility of finding another home and informing his companions. This information had become to think of our young people and in the meantime the water continued to flow as a source of a river despite attempts trying to stop, it was a failure and the pavement had become almost non-existent, fragmented, dislocated.

A few days later, during the night to an hour after midnight, they will be visited by men armed robbery. That night the young man remained with his young brother. His friend had gone to attend a birthday party of one of their former classmate and friend to his little brother went with their families for a family visit as usual every weekend.

These robbers knocked at the door on the pretext that they needed so that the pastor prays for a sick lady who was with them in critical condition. Responding to their request, their ABIBU says there is not a pastor who lives in this house may - be you have the wrong address, it would be best to look elsewhere. No, you lie to us, we know that there is a pastor who lives in the house they replied with an aggressive tone. But why do not you want to believe what I tell you!. Perhaps this pastor was my predecessor who is no longer here and I do not know where he lives, I'm a new tenant, then you go!

Once they change the pretext you refused to open the door because you keep wife of another man in your house, why you act this way, but we must enter into the house to investigate the case because we are the agents of the police mission in this house. This is the reason for our presence at your door. At the moment, his young brother blew his old brother not to open the door. Reflecting together, the two brothers agree on this decision. They replied saying we don't have a wife of another man in the house and if and only you hold your investigation, it would be better to wait until morning to enter in the house but this time, it n 'is not possible. As you insist to provide the door, we'll use strength, they responded!

At these words of intimidation, young men realized that they were dealing not with real policemen but the brigands, they took it seriously because they felt the danger and they answered them we understood that you came to us threatening, so you are not law enforcement officers. So whoever dare to open the door and enter the first in our house, we will die with him and know it well that it is men like you who live in this house, so prepare yourself accordingly because we're ready to face now!

These words are so crucial upset the attackers and they began to murmur among themselves, while posing several questions. Certainly it was moving in act or outright abandon their mission. Taking advantage of this moment of doubt between their bandit ABIBU exhorted his brother to keep their cool and do not panic. Once an idea came to him at the head of the emergency call and took the phone of his young brother that he used for cab service units that had it. He called his family and knowledge they come to their aid through the security service close to where they were.

Something said and done, after a few minutes, while the attackers continued to discuss an unknown number was a number of the Rapid Intervention Police called for clarification in report to where they were. After this conversation with the police unit on patrol, they heard a jeep coming at high speed and the area turned into a battlefield. The police battalion came to set Security victims exchanged blows balls with the gunmen, who took last flight. Overpowered the police and remained the situation until morning to protect victims. They took the opportunity to speak with the entire neighborhood and also establish their report to hand it to the hierarchy. Initially police, ABIBU glorified before God for having saved the hands of bandits. He then decides to leave the house determined on the same day for fear that the situation could turn sour with the decisive return of the attackers. That coincide with the return of his friend on Sunday morning, all unanimously hailed the decision ABIBU and went over to his execution.

As it was a Sunday, they sacrificed all participation in the Mass in favor of the move. They packed up all their stuff and they went in search of a means of transport that can hold all their belongings to the destination. Fortunately, they found a large vehicle that led up to her old sister who lived in a town near the periphery, while they the city center, so they were a little away from their old sister. Upon their arrival, they will be familiar very well received. Moreover, a room had been reserved for them, prepared for their stay.

Despite this welcome by many fellowship to his sister, her husband and their children, ABIBU do not always returned whenever he tried to think of these two adventures of the flood and the nocturnal visit by the robbers. Although there is space and comfort in its old sister, the young person does not feel his skin and also knowing his brother, a haughty character to make fun of people, he decided to home his maternal aunt, the younger their mother.

At night, before bed, he called his sister and he says: yaya, I really was flattered by the welcome that you have given us, thank you for this gesture, but I prefer to let my stuff here and I will of time to time to see them. Myself, I'll stay with the aunt until I find another new home and young brother could either choose to either stay here or follow me. This decision appeared to be reasonable face reality. Is not at all agree with his brother at the beginning of their conversation, but it ended up being convinced by the arguments of his brother.

The next day at work he spoke to his boss, who in turn expressed his compassion for the boy and encouraged him to stand firm. Having once heard the news, his aunt asked him to return home and disbursed way the next day. Upon his arrival in the evening, he went with his friend every day, he found his old room ready to receive them. This had arranged enchanted. Although everything was normal with the home of his maternal aunt, ABIBU had no ambition to stay long there because he did not want to stay in the family home and do not depend on anyone, as he already felt major and responsible.

It was time for him right down to jump higher as the sages say. The days passed, he was organized to bring together a new warranty and meanwhile he was tracking his former security with his former landlord, polygamous. This made him walk with unrealized promises. As he was tired and done with this old daddy, he solicited the help of his friend lawyer by training and profession to intervene in this matter. They stared at each appointment after talking they went to it. Speaking, the lawyer began by presenting to the landlord and his family. He followed these words as one who was your former tenant, this is my longtime friend who has suffered just to get his money back guarantee to you. My presence here is not justified by the same reason that you say?

My son, my son exclaimed the old Dad, I'm surprised you master your friend brings me here to this case lawyer money guarantee, why would you bring me to justice!

He excelled with beautiful words to stroke the young man but there failed because young people were determined to recover only guarantee not hear caress speech. Given the pressure and the determination of our young people, old dad went into the house and gave them the amount of the guarantee in question.

Having received the sum in question, in turn, strongly ABIBU thanked his lawyer friend and rewarded him with a sum as a recognition award. The rest he gave into the hands of one of his closest friends, unemployed for two years past, with the idea that this amount once placed in any gainful activity can yield profits can serve and help his friend unemployment to meet his needs. But alas, this was not the case unfortunately because that money had never been returned, under the pretext of a possible bankruptcy declared by fighter fight. Although it does not have enchanted, it could not be otherwise, if it was only to forgive him. This decision did not come only himself but also his other friends in the group of intimates.

Case decommissioned ABIBU sacrificed himself again to build its new warranty with on-board means. Alas, after a year, the warranty will be created. This time, he went to interest one of his colleagues, living in the neighborhood where he preferred to stay. Sympathetic to his young colleague of service, he brought in a Muslim believer commissioner with which he spoke well. While they were looking for the full house to rent, they found the other two commissioners with whom they talk about the same subject and they exchanged telephone contact. The young man was then pending appeals of these two groups of its new occasional contributors. Some time later, his phone rang. It was then the call from the other two commissioners, urging him to go to a house they had found in her neighborhood of choice.

But this offer was a scam, a stunt, a cabal, because these money hungry commissioners and experts in fraud, in complicity with a lady owner of a parcel, operate in this direction. Once aware of a market where someone needs a house to rent and the person falls into their hands. They talk with the lady so that bringing their victim that has no contradiction in their operation. The role of the lady would confirm the availability of the house. With the money received from victim›s hands, they share them to do their business with the idea to make a profit before the end of the submission of the applicant›s guarantee of the house. Here›s the scene:

As the phone rang, and picked ABIBU received the call of these two commissioners, informed him of the availability. They settled beyond the appointment in the evening when the young man will return to work, where they had seen for first time. The agreed time, the young man went straight to the meeting of these two crooks. Beyond they went to the plot was the house in question. At the entrance a lady met them outside the house just to the veranda. Speaking, one of two commissioners say ABIBU, this is the house where we were invited you to visit and the owner of the house is the lady who greeted us. Without much comment, I defer to the mother herself to say what she needs.

Courageous she was, she proceeded like any responsible home with questions to get a general idea and says her new tenant, she said: I want to know if you work or not and where? Your marital status? Single or married with many children. You come from where and how many people are you going to come and live occupy this house of two bedrooms and living room?

ABIBU replied: Mom, I work in a local company specifically in the city. I'm not married yet but I'm already engaged. I will stay with my brother and my two friends, we will total the number of four. My fiancee will from time to time to help us with housework.

Immediately, she responds, thank you my son for all these details, I hope it would be. This is the house that you intend to occupy. In principle i was bound to show you it inside, but because my husband before traveling I was recommended to get rid of his family, does not mean any member of his family that we would like to move but they are only surprises of the decision.

As they are now in the house, I invite you to an understanding and we will proceed in the following way: once you carry out your duty, I want to take this money to return to these commissioners to that they check a piece of our bedroom and living room where we'll live with my husband in his words, to avoid being encumbered by his family members. In fact, two days ago, our friends commissioners came to offer me a piece like lack of money in case I was not able to do something, but as we are in possession of it, i hope that in a month you would occupy the house, we trust issue.

Inexperienced, bewitched or what I say, ABIBU believing he was dealing with serious people, especially when he went into the plot, he found the lady with a bible on the table pretending someone who meditated on the word of God. He accepted everything that had been said by the lady. On the occasion, he poured the sum of rental guarantee through a lease established in the presence of these two commissioners, which forced the youth to complete the rest of the amount required by the mother the next day. To convince his fulfillment of the promise to complete the remaining warranty, he was forced to call his supervisor on the field for the realization of that promise.

Done deal, comes to the occupation of the house. ABIBU appeared as provided for in the day at his new lessor to inform him of his arrival in the hours that follow so that all arrangements are made for either side. Unfortunately, he did not find the lady and will be hosted by his daughter who was already a mother daughter. Also connected, enrolled in this game scam, she says: Sir, mom had moved for a prayer retreat to the hill organized by our church. Before her departure, she told me to convey the message that she had already found a home for us and we could go back to occupy the room to retire in two weeks. Besides, she has apologized for the disruption caused program regardless of its own will.

Disoriented, confused, upset, confused but calmed by these stroke words from the girl, the boy disbursed path despite himself, to wait for a new appointment. Two weeks later, he returned to see the lady but she was always absent on the pretext that the shepherd or pastor had extended retirement a few days but her daughter had sufficient precision, this time there the day of his return. One day by chance after so many days past full walk, he crossed the applicant that seeing the young man jumped and flickered by unexpected encounter.

She approached the boy while saying my son I've just returned, in fact I planned to call you tonight for you an appointment tomorrow afternoon so that your work has been talked about. Despite his anger is already drawn on his face, ABIBU accepted the appointment with a yellow smile. Along the way, he arrived at his friend who had been in contact with him and his crooks commissioner recounted the whole scene. In response his friend says, my dear friend, with everything you just tell me I am afraid that is a set up for you swindle your money. So be awake! Besides, tomorrow is paramount to me so I'll go with you instead of appointment and we all know what to do in this situation.

The next day he act accordance with the words of his friend and they went together to the lady, who was waiting with another new history, supposedly the son of his landlord, who lived in the house she would live, had crossed the other side of the neighbor country with the key, leaving in his stuff. He could come back in two weeks and as nobody can open this home with stuff of others in, may we wait all if possible!

After consulting with his companions, ABIBU very angry, he replied to his lessor: mom since we started this files, I've been too patient, too broad. I just heard back everything you just said, I prefer silent today and come back another day to draw the conclusion. Immediately he rose and invited his companion to follow. On the road of the house, his friend out feasibility concern over the scene he had just experienced. Without embage he recommends and urges his friend to be vigilant, because with the pace things are going he said: there is a risk that this case turns sour, where there is still time to take any other provisions.

Annoyed, upset, troubled by a situation in which he already feels victim. That day, the young man could not close the eye, but thanks to the advice of his relatives he tried. To cope with this situation, he went to alert his new lawyer friend. They make a strategy to deal with the lessor and his accomplices. They came to an agreement to meet with the lady on the day of the appointment, fearing that she can escape. They arrived as planned at the lessor, and they require shyly greeted the mother they go together to his landlord, for they realize also the veracity of the file so that they reap the consequences.

But the mother was not agreed not favorable under the pretext that it would be wrong for the fact that she would have involved other people. All this happened in the fishbowl of his accomplices, who came unwillingly, at the request of their client, who was charged to it. Who was not agreed, the master lawyer speaking while presenting, exhibiting his service card and said, as we did not agreed on this principle, in my capacity as defender of justice and attorney ABIBU, I recommend you give us back our guarantee with damages and interest for the time you have done work for this house in the opposite case the court awaits us, because tomorrow we will pick you complain. If you're not ready now with the money we pay, grace let us discharge that will be also signed by your accomplices agents.

Discharge in which you will specify that tomorrow we will get our own warranty. A fact accomplished, the lady replied while shaking my son, I'm sorry for what happened, instead we arrived at the court, I'd rather give you your money here. Taken by fear, she wanted to kneel down before them. Suddenly they act vigorously against the lady wanted to ask.

Talking again, the defender of law told him that he was not a question of love or worship anyone. As the key was to get the warranty, he brought the lady to the right. They authorized him to pay just the interest amount remitted without damage. Reaction salvation who arranged the lessor and she went immediately to get the money in the house to return to its rightful owner. Disappointed by the failure of two attempts and fraud related to the search of a home, the young boy become pessimistic in this regard, but he decided to continue his walk.

Shortly after, he enlisted in the adventure. This time, he sought the help of his old brother, the cousin family commissioner in another municipality. During his meeting with his cousin older than him, married and father of two children, gave him all the details in relation to the house he wanted to live. Setting to work, he went to a house by the way of his fellow commissioners. To get to bring the two parties on one side of the lessor and the other side its young brother the tenant, given the schedule of each. After several attempts, they eventually meet. That day was the first ABIBU arrived at the place of appointment, accompanied by his cousin and his followers. All the expectations of the lessor at his home, which arrived last.

Already knowing the reason for its visitors, the man received them in African. He immediately defer to one of the commissioners present at this place. Speaking latter introduise himself while exhibiting all the world, because it was he who done the deck for the success of this folder. Speaking in turn, the landlord will say a few days ago that my friend here I had spoken to you and we are finally realizing this file. But at first, let me call the tenant who occupies up to this said house, for he actually confirmed its release and we will continue our conversation later. On his appearance, he expressed the desire to free home warranty provided it is returned and that he will get another room elsewhere.

After this statement, he withdrew from the group to continue to wander about their business. They concluded the file while setting an appointment after a month, until the current occupant releases the house and the landlord to make the small work arrangement of the plot and the house. Accustomed to adventures donors, one week before the date fixed for ABIBU passed to realize the reality on the ground. To his surprise, he finds that nothing was done and the big house occupied by the so-called donor was already occupied by another family. Astonished, upset the young man did not understand.

A few minutes later, he approached and asked the lady found mending her stuff of the house, saying politely, please madam, I apologize for the inconvenience. After introducing himself, he asked her if it was the same family as the landlord. No, says the lady, we are also his new tenants. Moreover it is last night she said that we had occupied the house after our pressure, because the deadline had already expired fixed; come we were also threatened beyond where we lived, that why we have also lobbied until he finished it last night as to move with his family. Despite this, we are undergoing another by pressure of his family not recognize our lease, supposedly that the parcel is being sold and that he could not commit to such a contract without consulting the more especially it is a simple manager. Do you know his current address says the boy! No replied the lady, go ask the other tenants that we found here, perhaps they are better placed to answer this question. It does not interest us too.

ABIBU turned toward the neighbor, that is to say, the tenant should give him the house. By approaching the young man asked the question whether the person was ready to release the house. The gentleman replied, not because he expected that it surrenders its guarantee he never recover until these days. This reply shook once more the boy. Exclaimed, oh it's true!

He immediately pulled out his phone and tried to call his landlord, unfortunately the phone was closed. So without further action. By this, the boy understood it was again being defrauded. At the end of the plot, he went straight to his cousin to inform him of the situation. Also surprised by this adventure, he suggested his young to keep his calm so that they arrive to conduct investigations calmly.

Embarrassed, shocked, hurt his heart by this new adventure which he was again victim ABIBU informed his own including his older sister with whom he had filed his stuff and housed two days before he went to his aunt kindergarten, where he was these days, including his friend the lawyer, his companion these circumstances. Approaching all his people, he would not only consolation, but the solution to this particular problem.

Given the severity of this problem by the disappearance of his landlord without a trace, all unanimously offered him to go complain to the police near the area where Dad lived missing. That day, the young man was accompanied by a police officer, his brother and his friend lawyer. They filed the complaint through wholes costs related to the filing. After having listened to the record, the judicial officer promised their dad's arrest this within 48 hours. And he advised them not to close their telephones for fear that it might create prejudice to the file. The three companions returned with the hope that the promise will be carried out as promised.

But to their surprise, nothing was done, that is to say they have not received any phone call from the police station for two days. When they returned to them, they replied that they had not yet evidence and the investigation was ongoing and they asked another motivation. This application does not enchanted. Reacted then: we have paid all the expenses that we restored to our rights, but so far we do not even have a favorable response to our request, you ask us to pay yet another fee, is that is honest?. first do your work and the rest we will see later. This reaction did not help the police, but they accepted despite themselves.

When they parted from them, the police officer, brother to ABIBU these fellow officers suspected a certain flexibility and a certain complicity. He informed his two companions and even suggested that they should investigate themselves. This proposal will be well received by the group and they began to reflect on the feasibility, implementation or carrying out this idea.

They came to an agreement to sacrifice a whole day. This could allow them to roam, searching information, but the lawyer should avoid this operation because it was difficult for him to find a free day as proposed. Despite this, he encouraged them to do so while remaining in constant contact. At the day agreed ABIBU asked permission from his boss that he will be absent the next day and he gave him no problem. Moreover, he had even received the support of his boss. This gesture from his leader urged more responsibility. As they were in possession of some traces or clues to the address of the second wife of the person, the church where he prays, the school attended by one of his children. They stared appointments around the home of that woman. The time of the appointment was 6:00. Wholes its arrangement was done by phone because they do not live together. One of the periphery and the other almost downtown. Taking their word, they both arrived almost at the same time and they began the operation. Surprised to see the police commander in civilian clothes ABIBU asked him: I thought commander held in police see you, but why choose it?

Replied the officer, usually when we go for such inspection mission, it is recommended advisable worn civilian clothing to avoid attracting the attention of people. At the finish of this answer, he lifted his jacket a little while showing him his revolver and a pair of craquât. With this demonstration, the young man thought and soothes.

Accustomed to such circumstances, the commander directs the operation with a strategy or plan that was presented in the following way: they should first be placed in the corner of the street near the home of his second wife to monitor the wholes movements into and out of the plot. If they observed anything, then they should go to church just before the end of morning Mass, as he used to go to Mass every morning according to the information available to them. In case of failure, they should finally lead to the school of one of his children, the spinning far he could go. This operation was scheduled for the entire day.

As the first two attempts failed, they took the direction of the school. Upon their arrival, they will not be welcomed with school authorities because they had qualified this approach illegal despite all the explanations provided by the investigators. They complicated their life while treating the kidnappers. That is to say, as specialists kidnapping. They asked them to conduct investigations outside the school.

Have not found successful in their three targets, they decided to return to the starting point, which was around the home of the second wife. Just when it began to get dark, at sunset they came up the gentleman in question and entered the said parcel. Relieved by their presence, they entered themselves in the same plot as they walked and straight in front of the lady. By tapping at the door, a lady came out to greet them and answer their question.

Yes, what can I do for you, she responds. Hello lady, we came to see the head of the house, they reacted. Having no answer for them, especially that they did not come, she returned to the house to inform her old sister, the wife in, which will in turn realize personally visitors. Wanting to do the same as her sister, the result is the same. The response from the lady will be so negative. That is to say that her husband was not at home.

To move forward, the two visitors will eventually arise. But on their side, they remained adamant because they did say the truth. Annoyed by this attitude, the commander out his claws and said while presenting: as you do not tell us the truth, even as we enter we saw while we were waiting outside for several hours, it is sufficient proof a certain complicity. On the occasion he gave them his true identity of the police officer, while showing them everything he had for this mission.

This presentation will upset the ladies, they began to speak in their dialect, while crying. Commander thundered loudly and told them we did not come to attend any show, but we just need your husband. As trolling, I call our first mobile jeep to come search the house. In case the man is caught, you too will be involved in this case as her accomplices. So you'll also be arrested.

Please commander, does not so, may we find a solution together, said the lady. Dad has just arrived and it is taking a rest, we'll call it right away to come your way. Once said, Dad quietly out of his house and began to apologize to our guests for the inconvenience. After making us walk by your disappearance, replied ABIBU, you still have the audacity to hold such things!

Continuing his sentence, dad today we came only recover our money, otherwise it is justice whose will decide. Trying to convince his visitors, trying to give them explanations. This was a waste of time and they resorted to the same police station to which the complaint was filed. Half an hour after four policemen sent laid hands on with Lessor criminal cracked hand curated destination. As they went to the police station in question, knowing his adventures, the locals laughed at him and booing him, while shouting: hi, hi, hi, thief, crook, it is shameful for a dad this age to conduct such a life. Please punish him severely.

Arrival at the police station, the police officer should hear on the record. He then called the complainant and the accused. When asked by the officer if he could find the solution to their problem or negotiate without their intervention. Not replied vigorously complainant, referring an American adage, he said: we do not negotiate with pirates because we had too walk. Wanting to beg the young man for a possible negotiation but it ended in failure.

The officer executed the complainant's decision and called the police put the guard to escort the accused to the place of detention, commonly called "the dungeon." That for a period of 72 hours beyond the deadline, said the officer, he will be transferred to the prosecution to be sent to the Central Prison. The lessor criminal could escape from it all by paying or reimbursing the rental guarantee its tenant with an almond complainant paid to the police. ABIBU left the place after half relieved because although the man was arrested, but has not yet recovered his money, which was his main concern.

To exit the humiliating situation that had arrived, the family of the father was mobilized to raise the money that had been required to pay, and especially to prevent their father, husband and brother did not go to the central prison, where where things can be more complicated. After two days, they gave the ¾ of the amount due, and having no other alternative, they begged the boy to ask for a pardon. That give him what they had found in their hands with the guarantee of a radio, the remaining amount as equivalent mortgaged they can recover on payment of the remaining amount in a reasonable time. This negotiation was to release a first step the inmate. Animated by a human sense, accepted the ABIBU proposal. They went all the police, he ordered the release of its protagonist who thanked all his heart. The day fixed for the reckoning came, the family accused appears with the rest of the money and the young man in turn, sends them on the radio.

With all the expenses incurred to end this story, the boy was left with 2/3 of the initial amount. From where he was obliged to seek yet to complete its guaranteed price of many sacrifices. Identify, engage in the project, the amount will be finally established. Abandoning his cousin, he confided to his former agent, Pastor get him again for a house to rent according to their preferences. As soon as the pastor began to work, but during this period, the houses of this caliber were not made to see.

Although asked to wait, the commission offered him alternatives such as bedroom and living room. Anxious to find a house to break the addiction, who already felt responsible, he finally accepted the proposal. Having agreed he was invited by his collaborator the pastor to visit a house in the neighborhood that he would not live. As a fact was accomplished, he accepted despite him pay the money to the owner, who was one of the heirs of each plot and each of them had his door he ran his own volition. Either personally or by occupying making rent. That time his landlord was the penultimate of the family with whom he poured out his rental guarantee.

It was then that the commissioner organized the ceremony or meeting of the lease, which met the landlord and the tenant. A few days later, the boy, making a turn to account the evolution of things, he discovers that his cousin is a smoker lessor and seller of hemp. This is the one with whom he will live and not live as their elder also not the plot, it is the man who ran all hemp immediate problems. The so-called responsible had built a shack in the middle of two buildings located in their plot. One of his older brothers who was seriously ill occupied a room on the first building. In this same house was also a bedroom and living room, occupied by his two sisters and their children, all girls. The other two are were occupied by tenants, including ABIBU was there. To clear the first building was the house left by their parent, where the family lived. It was a house that had an entrance that led directly to the living room surrounded. After the death of their father and from mother to his country of origin. The children had seen fit to change the house, which had only one entry in each four-door was a small room, which could contain three plastic chairs, a shelf and a small bedroom with a double bed could not be installed.

As the plot there were two houses and a shack, the other house had only two doors, all occupied by tenants. This house was built by the first and second daughter of the family, which also no longer lived in the plot, she had followed their mother in her native country. The lessor and the lessor co-boy was older than him and had almost his age. All tenants he saw there were all married with children and there were even those in the same room and living room, which also housed their cousins, nephews and nieces, and even parents and step-parents. That is to say, they also lived with other members of their extended family to share their own home.

During the first visit ABIBU in the plot, he had noticed that the sanitary facilities were not viable, posing the problem, he promised to arrange for his landlord before the deadline for him to come take the house. Because according to the process or its preparations were in court. ABIBU had trusted brother and therefore that future pastor of a church revival in the area. On the eve of the day when the young man should hold the job after he feasibility of a round the place to see if the house was released, so it sends the painter do his job. But this was not the case because unfortunately nothing was done and moving and sanitary facilities.

Wanting to know why, his landlord tells him that there was a problem where it would enter the door and the window he had set were not yet ready. As for sanitation facilities, they awaited the watchword of their great brother who was suffering these days. Knowing donors starting from his little experience in this field and to end the event or reason advanced by it, ABIBU called and fixed an appointment with her carpenter to help the landlord. He informed directly, while also stating that all the carpenter work will be as under its own load. That is to say, had nothing to pay.

This commitment was as the foundation to move forward on the side of the lessor that the young man was beginning to suspect. The next day the carpenter came and the work was completed done as planned. On the evening of the same day, the landlord was forced to move because there was no reason he can remember. And the boy held the hand of his home the next day after finishing all the work of painting, plastering and many other related before normal occupancy of a new home.

Although nothing was done at a hygienic facilities, he decided nevertheless to inhabit the land. At night, he settled with one of his two younger brothers. In the morning, as if was a Saturday holiday for ABIBU, he had allowed to recover his property that were far from his great sister. A week after installation, these donors were tested, their brother was seriously ill and died the body was kept in the morgue. Time for them to prepare the funeral.

Since that day, their family members come to spend night in the plot. They are allowed to move around even before the doors of tenants without authorization. They worried about anything because the land belonged to them. The day of the funeral watched as the body was out, there was more space following arrangements and facilities made to make the final tribute to his.

That evening, the young man found himself between the hammer and the anvil. Not wanting to spend the entire night ensured that, given what he had to do the next day and could not sleep in his house, not just noises of all kinds, but especially fear of dealing with wholes evils. So he opted to stay with them for a while until the late hours and thereafter to eclipse last night to spend around a hotel. Hereafter he will directly go about their daily business. After this is over, the life took his right path. ABIBU should adapt to the realities of the field and the neighborhood. Compared to the plot, he should carry a small bucket with which he would use especially great need. To do so without too upset neighbors, he took advantage to do while he was bathing. And at the end of the shower, they should pay into the hole of the toilet tank already ruined.

As for the neighborhood, this medium was considered a red zone because there were many thieves. This created a total insecurity especially at night. But there were times during the day when we attended shows young brigands them, which by the way, raided, breaking stories people or even hurt them. The only way to deal with these two major problems was that of adaptation for sanitary facilities and care for the insecurity in the area. Then the young man chose to do that instead of much needed service on weekdays and weekends he used the formula of the small bucket.

Versus insecurity, it was organized too late to do back home. That is to say, not to exceed 21 hours away from home. While at home, the door was still closed, but the two open windows because they were unpatriotic sow disorder even during the day into the plots of others.

As the days and months with no solution from its donors, ABIBU already thought the move. And he began again to save for a new guarantee, which is more consistent than the old. He did not want to talk about it in advance to the landlord of his house to be put in commission, and especially to prevent the move is under pressure. The law also stipulates that once your warranty is returned, you are obliged to vacate the house for a term not to penalize somebody else.

Wise he was, he kept silent until he had found a new home in the neighborhood where he began to be a tenant. A neighborhood favorite for him, because he almost filled the conditions he wanted. While he was preparing to leave his old home for a new one, after announcing its donors, who were surprised at the news came the time of negotiation. On the one hand, he negotiated the date of occupation of the new house on the other side, he negotiated his move. All this should not exceed two weeks. Meanwhile, he also negotiated with respect to goods that could not be moved or for compensation in nature or with money. If the ceiling, cover-curtains, lamp tubes, bulbs, sockets and switch. Two parallel approaches ended in success.

The day he had recovered the key to his new home, he told his deputy to come and collect his own the next day. To perform the move, he asked the help of his two younger brothers, cousins from the maternal side including his two young brothers of his fiance or bride because this time ABIBU had associated with the choice of a new home. He acted as not only to give value to his bride, but because she was the first person to push her lover to leave this environment.

Despite the heavy rain that had rained that day in the morning in the city, the young man, determined to move that same day, he did not shrink this obstacle rain, he and his companions began to carry stuff home with the man's cart. The carriage man was one of the old brothers to the landlord, who was questioned by a police officer who had caught doing his work beyond the hours permitted by law. Knowing the intention of the police to calm the situation after a discussion, the boy slipped a penny to the police. The case was decommissioned and closed as it was the last lap of transporting goods, moving endind the same night.

Tired wholes these movements, they spent all night in the lounge with the stuffs. The next morning, as it was the weekend, they contrived and put order into this new house. The first impressions of his new home seemed to be good, because the plot was tightly closed primarily with sanitation facilities can meet the standards. But his concern was focused on the behavior of his landlord and his family.

Wanting to make a comparison with its previous home, he realizes that his there was to eat and drink. By the fact that he would live in the same plot with the mother and the family of his donor. That family consisted of his mother and her five sisters who each have more than one child, all in a three-piece living room and bedroom. Meanwhile his landlord, was tenant also somewhere. The house occupied ABIBU contained two bedrooms and living room and other rooms occupied tenants each had a bedroom and a living room. Beside this was a studio occupied by a young couple whose improvised concubine was already pregnancy.

One day returning from work, as he watched the reality of this plot, he sees his mother coming lessor of the same generation as her grandmother, approached him while asked for a chat in his house. After inviting him to sit down, he began to listen her with his fiancee, who was at his side. Speaking, the old lady said, my son, my presence here among you, is nothing other than to share with you the realities of my plot. Briefly she spoke of her family to finally forever more on the lives of its tenants, who she often tried sows, disorders and conflicts in the plot. To do this, she recommended to the engaged couple not to get too attached to their fellow tenants, lest they also do not fall into this trap. In response the couple thanked the old lady for all the information and she left.

This visit gave idea for thought to the engaged couple. To properly conduct investigations in relation to the behavior of each other, they all take off until they realized the true reality, that: the side of tenants, there was a certain meanness spirit that characterized, they form friendships to peddle against the family of the donor. This family was seen as the scapegoat for their problems coming. With the presence of their brother crippled, a troubled young boy mind and their girls do not marry, but only have children in the same plot without responsible husbands. These realities reflected sufficiently, according to tenants, the existence of witchcraft in this family.

On the other side of the donor's family, confused, disorganized and characterized by a lack of discipline, accusing tenants mock them through their conversation and meeting. So there was no waiting between landlords and tenants. Faced with these realities, and his bride ABIBU decided not to meddle in their conflict. They took part of any group. Moreover, they had no direct contact with one of them, but they were on good terms with everyone. And to avoid falling into their trap, this young couple, his brother and their visitors prefer to spend their day in their house more than outside. A behavior that was enjoyed by both groups protagonists, each seeking to turn to approach him for advice.

The young man in turn, by his wisdom, knowledge and intelligence are gradually preparing to go live in a other he had experienced. A framework that can enable it to ensure survival and a good education for his future home, starting with his fiancee and their children they will have in the long run. Thus ABIBU devoted himself to his project and not family that described himself in futility.

Although the boy was determined to live a much more peaceful than the center where he lived, to ensure the safety of his future home and the education of his children. He will again be disappointed by the attitude of the family of their new landlord. This one was his service colleague. Two weeks after his marriage, the young man moved with his wife to the city center for the hectic town outskirts of the city, accompanied by his young brother.

When they arrived in the land, they found that nothing had been done as agreed with his colleague from service, his new landlord. They would occupy the house was not released. They found the two younger brothers of his colleague quietly occupied the room. By asking them if they were aware of their arrival. No, they replied. It is from there ABIBU had understood that there was something that was not his friend between lessor and other members of his family. Confused, he tried to join his friend on the phone lessor, unfortunately it was unavailable due to lack of support.

While they were trying to find a solution to this misunderstanding, the person will appear. After negotiating behind closed doors with his brothers. They came to the conclusion that the house should be transferred to the lessee at the moment. But it will be partially occupied, that is to say, a bedroom and living room will be occupied by them and another room in which were the affairs of his young sister could remain temporarily closed until the rest of the their warranty is paid by their tenants. Meanwhile, young sister could occasionally go to ensure his property. That day as it was already late, the couple could not be tenant night in their new home, saw the movement and preparations for the removal of their donors. They went to sleep in the great ABIBU who lived nearby and stayed there on their property instead.

The next morning, they came to prepare their home and they settled there. A day after they spent two months as they gradually pay the remainder of the warranty, they come see the young sister of his friend lessor as usual. She entered the house precisely in her room and arrange his stories. Curiously at her output, the young man noticed that the room was not locked as usual. He informed his wife and their neighbor with whom they conversed in the verandah. The two ladies reacted saying maybe she forgot to close, question to inform her young brother with whom we live, so he also informs turn to his sister.

A few hours later, around 20 hours, that person happens again and she went straight to her room. Addressing her ABIBU say we thought you forgot to lock your room. She replied saying no, it was a way to indicate that I was still there. Immediately the next tenant pair of the young man, the girl informed the pastor, another neighbor tenant wanted to meet her. Reacting she: ok, thank you for the information, we may meet tomorrow, because I'm tired and I want to spend night here. Surprised by these statements, all became confused. They talk to each other tenants. Sleep here, that is to say, share the same room with the tenants that we are! It was not possible! This is absurd! This is an abomination! They laid them as many questions tenants.

Despite their outrage, concern, question and wonder the situation remained intact because the girl actually spent the night with the couple and although they try mediation of her old brother, who begged his tenants tolerance so that the next day a solution is found to the mutable. That night the couple accepted the offer with great difficulty and hardly slept.

In the morning, the girl's brothers including their old brother conspired together to condemn the act committed by their sister. But it does nothing to worried and continued her three days as expected. As they came to convince their sister to change he decision, the three brothers turned to their tenant, so he accepts this, saying please accept her as your sister who is visiting from you because that we are already a family.

Speaking, the woman not wanting ABIBU also understand, told them as your sister wants to stay there for three days without taking into account other parameters, although we have not yet completed the remaining warranty. It is posing as an act is an abomination. Knowing that we are a couple, humanly and with respect to our sacred union like an African Christian and in addition, she did not do so. Therefore, it would be better if we leave the whole house until the day of her departure, we will come back, because we are african, it is a sacrilege.

This intervention upset the three brothers. They were faced with a accomplish fact and they begged their new tenants, so that they do overflow. Finally account their interlocutors understand and eventually agreed that the girl ends her stay with them.

Shortly after this unfortunate incident, before the deadline agreed for the settlement of account, that is to say, to satisfy the debt by the tenant, which will result as the release of the second chamber by donors. ABIBU received a phone call from his colleague and lessor will say my dear friend, my sister wants to go in a few days to settle there permanently. To do this, I need this money left as soon as possible to prepare for her return. If you can prepare this amount because we are already at the end of the month. In response, ABIBU replied with these words: "My dear friend, how can you do so because you entant as a worker and knowing our professional realities, the end of the month, professional language is not necessarily the last day of the month, but the first five days next month. If your sister does not know this is up to you to mean her. I know I owe you that amount by the end of the current week, the time that I was sending my salary above that it must come from another province. So a quite patience."

But his landlord did not seem to understand his explanations and he insisted on doing its best to solve that problem. They separated in this misunderstanding. About confused by his landlord, friend and colleague ABIBU decided to remedy this situation, the risk of recall its new leaders, if they could send him his wages. The reaction of his direct superior was not long, though it has been positive, but it was followed by a reprimand, which failed to lose his new job.

Two days after his salary was half of his net salary for nimble only 15 days of the month, has been come. Given the inadequacy of the amount sent his wife again in order to end this case the warranty offered her husband to take her jewels to her sale. The husband executed with just the request of his wife. With this amount gained from the sale of these gold jewelry, they met the amount in question and the rest, they use it for other purposes.

They called their landlord to give him the remainder of the warranty. On arrival, the couple showed their discontent with the person, while advising him to tell his brothers and sisters, they said, life will bring a lot of surprises, therefore it would be prudent to treat relationships because things can change one day as they are today because you consider that today can become landlord tenant of the land where you will be tomorrow tenant.

With their two neighboring tenants including one married with a two year old daughter and another pastor of a revival church unmarried but betrothed was a climate of peace that allowed everyone took care of his home. After a few months of living together, ABIBU noticed something was wrong in the sense of organization in the plot, he suggested a meeting between just men. The day of the meeting the three men retreated one evening and they talked about problems relating to the organization of the plot in which they praise namely: daily maintenance of sanitation facilities, improving the quality of electricity constitutes a problem in this area and the time payment of electricity bills and water. But the application of what was said, was a problem starting with donors themselves to the tenants. Donors in the camp, they said that it does not concern them. Cleaning turns hygienic and other facilities were not their affair, especially since this idea is coming from tenants, it had nothing to do with them.

They continued saying their tenants had not given them a moral lesson. For them they could not execute a decision from their old brother ABIBU friend. Tenants in the camp, and their wives as they also say that after having observed and executed what has been said, so donors refused all new directives issued at the meeting. This became a tip for women in these three tenants to stop maintaining sanitary facilities. Men as their side were discouraged to continue with their plan to make the plot area.

As a result each tenant with a fireplace retreated home and began to act according to his good sense. Although they kept a good climate in the plot, but no one could take the initiative to meet others. Since that day the couple understands and concluded that «the lessor is not a friend of the tenant and vice versa.» Where everyone has an interest in his guard, lest we be disappointed in one way or another.

The End.

Printed in the United States
By Bookmasters